Julia grabbed a purpl... ...o the banana. She lifted the banana into the air and waved it like a flag. Naturally it broke in two and fell to the floor. Julia stretched out her arm. "Gimme!"

"You can't eat it now," I said. "It's dirty."

"Want nana!" she whined. "Want nana!"

"How about a bread stick?" I suggested, handing her one.

"No!" she cried, batting it away.

"Try some creamed spinach," Jackson suggested, offering her a spoonful.

She swatted at the spoon, which sent the spinach flying. It landed with a plop on Jackson's cheek. "Yuck!" he wailed.

I started to laugh, but stopped when Julia shoved the plate containing the collapsed celery-stick skyscraper off the table. It clattered to the floor, throwing wads of peanut butter everywhere.

"I give up!" I shouted. "This is a disaster!"

Spinach
with Chocolate Sauce

Francess Lantz

If you purchased this book without a cover, you should be aware that this book is stolen property. It was reported as "unsold and destroyed" to the publisher, and neither the author nor the publisher has received any payment for this "stripped book."

Copyright © 1997 by Francess Lantz.

Cover illustration by Paul Casale.
Copyright © 1997 by Troll Communications L.L.C.

Published by Troll Communications L.L.C.

All rights reserved. No part of this book may be reproduced or utilized in any form or by any means, electronic or mechanical, including photocopying, recording, or by any information storage and retrieval system, without written permission from the publisher.

Printed in the United States of America.

10 9 8 7 6 5 4 3 2 1

For Terry Ray,
who understands about child stars,
good food, and fun

Chapter
1

"Uck! Uck! What doing, Uck?"

The sound of my two-year-old sister's voice set off a warning siren inside my head. *Toddler alert! Toddler alert!*

Quickly, quietly, I ran to my bedroom door and peeked out. There was Julia padding down the hall, dragging her tattered baby doll, Loola, behind her. The two of them had already been to visit me once this morning, at 6 A.M. to be exact. That's when Julia woke me up by tugging on my eyelashes and shouting, "Sun's up, Uck!" in my ear.

I guess I should explain right now that my name isn't really Uck. It's Puck, but Julia can't say the letter *P* very well, or many other letters either. Mom says that's perfectly normal for a kid her age, but it's kind of embarrassing when she calls me Uck in public. Like the time Mom and Julia came to pick me up after school and Julia announced, loud enough for the entire schoolyard to hear, "I make a oop. You make oop, Uck?"

Since then, not a day goes by that someone in my class doesn't ask me, "You make a oop today, Uck?" Then everyone laughs themselves silly and I wonder for the billionth time why Mom and Dad decided to give me a baby sister for my tenth birthday, instead of something useful like a new bike helmet, or maybe a snake.

"Uck, want to play dolls?" Julia called from the hallway.

Was she kidding? What I wanted to do was read the latest issue of *Mountain Bike Monthly*, but there was no hope of that with Julia around. So I grabbed the mag, dropped to my stomach, and scooted under my bed. The dust balls were the size of golf balls, and the smell coming from my sneakers could suffocate a horse, but I didn't care. I held my breath and waited.

"Uck?" she called, walking into my room. "Where Uck?"

Go away, I said silently, watching her little feet toddle across the carpet. *Go see what Mom and Dad are doing.*

No such luck. She picked up one of my old socks from the floor and began to suck on it thoughtfully. *Okay,* I thought, *if that's the way it's going to be, I'll just wait you out.*

I reached for *Mountain Bike Monthly* and quietly opened it. There was an ad for the new Cheetah 2000 on the inside cover, the one with the V-shaped frame, Sun Dog derailleurs, and Thumper XT suspension and shocks. I closed my eyes and imagined myself rocketing down the hill behind my house on my new Cheetah 2000. I pictured myself swerving around a boulder, catching air, and landing in a cloud of dust. Awesome!

Julia's tiny nasal voice brought me back to the present. "Here, Loola," she said. "Your turn now."

Your turn for what? I wondered. I lifted the blanket that was draped over the edge of my bed and peered out. Oh, no! Julia had opened my container of fish food and was flinging handfuls of it into the air. It wafted slowly to the ground like smelly confetti.

"See, Loola," Julia cried happily, "it snowing!"

I hesitated, uncertain whether to leap up and grab the fish food out of her hot little hands or bite my tongue and wait to see if she got bored and left. At that moment, she turned around and addressed the fish. "Here, fishies. Breakfast for *oo*." She climbed onto the milk crate that held my baseball cards and raised the container of fish food over the tank.

"Stop!" I screamed.

But it was too late. Julia turned over the container, and about six months' worth of fish food fell into the tank. The fish took one look and went nuts. It was as if a freeze-dried whale had just fallen from heaven.

I rolled out from under the bed, grabbed the net beside the tank, and scooped up most of the fish food. Then I turned to Julia. "Get out of my room!" I shouted, pointing at the door.

"Hi, Uck," she said pleasantly. "Me feed fishies. See?" She thrust her hand into the tank and grabbed at a passing angel fish. Water sloshed across the bookcase.

"That's it," I said angrily, scooping up Julia and carrying her down the hall like a sack of potatoes. "You're out of here."

Julia let out a shriek that made our basset hound, Pepperoni, throw back his head and howl. I glanced down at him as I passed through the living room. "Think how *I* feel," I muttered.

Julia was kicking, scratching, and twisting like a wild animal, but I carried her into the kitchen and deposited her at my parents' feet. She stopped screaming and reached down to examine a crumb on the floor. "Can't a guy have a moment's peace around here?" I demanded.

Mom looked up from the bowl of pinkish glop she was stirring. "Taste this," she said, thrusting a spoonful in my direction.

I took a tentative lick. "Not bad. What is it?"

"Sour cream with caviar, capers, and a touch of anchovy paste," Dad replied. "Imagine it dribbled over poached salmon on a bed of red cabbage." He grinned. "Another masterpiece from the kitchen of Chef Rosen!"

Let me explain about my parents. Mom and Dad are total food fanatics (which explains why they named me after well-known Los Angeles chef Wolfgang Puck, and my sister after the famous TV cooking show host Julia Child). Both of them have spent most of their lives working in restaurants—Mom as a chef, and my father as a waiter and, later, a maitre d'. During the past year, they had both been working at a pricey Beverly Hills restaurant called Table Manners. The restaurant—and they—recently had been given a glowing review in *American Gourmet* magazine, which meant they had suddenly become extremely famous.

Famous? you're probably thinking. *A chef and a maitre d'?* Well, yes. That's because in Los Angeles, where we live, eating out is a way of life. Movie stars and other Hollywood types think nothing of spending hundreds of dollars for a meal at the latest hip, trendy cafe. Around here, restaurants aren't just places to consume food; they're places to network, make deals, see people, and be seen. That's why restaurants like Table Manners are booked months in advance, and why some people will do almost anything just to get a reservation.

But right then I had other things on my mind besides food. Like Julia. "Can't you keep that creature on a leash?" I asked, pointing down at her. "She's a menace."

"That creature is your sister," Mom replied. "If she's bothering you, why don't you lock your door?"

"Because then she stands outside and screams until I can't hear myself think."

"Buh-boo," Julia announced, climbing the rungs of one of the counter stools. "Want buh-boo." The stool began to tip over, and Dad had to lunge forward to steady it.

"Down, little monkey," he said, lowering her to the floor. "No more bottles for you. You're a big girl now." He handed her a toddler cup filled with apple juice, but she batted it to the floor.

"Buh-boo!" she wailed. "Want buh-boo!"

Mom shook her head. She and Dad had been trying to wean Julia from her bottle for weeks now, but the little monster was having none of it. To listen to her howl, you'd think those dopey bottles were the only thing that made life worth living.

"Did you do your homework, Puck?" Dad asked, trying to ignore Julia's breathless sobs.

Homework? How could a guy think about homework at a time like this? Summer vacation started in less than a week, and my best friend, Jackson, and I planned to spend the summer exploring the hillsides and canyons behind our houses on our mountain bikes. There were miles and miles of trails we hadn't ridden yet, plus a dry creek bed we were dying to follow. But first we had to get our bikes tuned up—or better yet, think up a way to get our hands on a couple of brand-new Cheetah 2000s.

"Can I go over to Jackson's house?" I asked, leaning against the counter and giving my parents a pleading look. "I've only got a couple of pages of math. I can whip them off before dinner."

"No can do," Dad replied. "Jacques just called. There's an emergency staff meeting at noon. We need you to watch Julia till we get back."

I let out a groan. Jacques Brouchard was the owner of Table Manners. It seemed like he was always calling emergency staff meetings, usually because some snobby celebrity had complained about the food or the service.

Julia was still whining. "Buh-boo!" she cried, pulling at Dad's pant leg. "Want buh-boo!" She threw herself down on the floor and held her breath.

"Good heavens, look!" Mom gasped. "Her face is turning blue!"

"I don't care what the pediatrician says," Dad exclaimed, reaching down to pick up Julia. "I can't take this screaming."

"Oh, what the heck," Mom shouted, holding her ears. "One bottle can't hurt her." She grabbed the toddler cup, poured the contents into a bottle, and handed it to Julia. Instantly my sister stopped sobbing and started sucking.

"No fair!" I protested. "She holds her breath for two seconds and you give in. Maybe I should throw a tantrum every time I want something." I pounded my fists against the counter. "I want to go to Jackson's house! I want to go to Jackson's house!"

"Not funny," Dad said sternly. "You're twelve years old. Julia is just a baby."

"We'll talk about this later," Mom said, taking off her chef's apron and tossing it on a stool. "We'll be home in an hour, Puck. Two at most. Take out the poached salmon when the timer rings, okay?"

So much for going to Jackson's house. I glanced over at Julia, who had finished the bottle and was chasing Pepperoni through the living room. As they rounded the coffee table, she knocked my new mountain bike video, *Downhill Demons,* onto the floor, then tripped and landed on it with a crunch. I let out a sigh. It was going to be a long afternoon.

By the time Mom and Dad got home, Julia had flushed my mother's eyeliner down the toilet, squeezed a tube of toothpaste into the tub, and jammed Play-Doh into my bicycle chain. After that last offense, I had been tempted to fling her off the back deck into the prickly pear cactus. But when my parents walked through the front door and I saw their shell-shocked faces, I forgot all about Julia.

"What happened this time?" I asked. "Did Sylvester Stallone find a hair in his salad dressing or something?"

"Worse," Mom said glumly. "Much worse."

"Jacques is closing the restaurant," Dad said. "As of today your mother and I are out of a job."

"Closing the restaurant?" I cried. "But why?"

"Jacques just found out his business manager has been stealing from him," Mom said. "He's broke, his creditors are taking him to court, and the IRS claims he owes them half a million dollars."

"Can you believe it?" Dad asked, scooping up Julia, who had appeared at the end of the hall wearing nothing but her socks. "One minute we're the toast of Hollywood, the next minute we're unemployed."

"Don't worry," I said. "You can get another job, no problem. Restaurants will be lining up to hire you."

"I suppose," Mom replied, plopping down on the living room couch. "I just wish we had more control over our lives. We're always at the mercy of some temperamental restaurant owner who thinks he knows more about food than we do."

"Remember that guy you worked for back in ninety-two?" Dad asked. "Just because the restaurant was named Cilantro he thought you had to put cilantro in everything, even the desserts."

Mom chuckled and shook her head. "Someday we're going to open our own restaurant and do things *our* way."

Dad didn't answer. He was staring out the picture

window at the wispy white clouds floating over the Hollywood Hills. Then suddenly, he turned to Mom. "Let's do it."

"Do what?"

"Open our own restaurant."

Mom laughed. "It's a wonderful fantasy, but we don't have the money."

Dad shrugged. "So we'll borrow some. With our reputation, we shouldn't have any trouble getting a loan."

"I don't know," Mom said skeptically. "You know how unpredictable the restaurant scene is in this town. If we open a place and it doesn't catch on instantly, we could lose everything."

"Look, you guys," I said, picturing Mom and Dad standing at a freeway entrance holding a sign that said WILL WORK FOR FOOD, "don't do anything crazy."

"A restaurant of our own isn't crazy—not if we come up with a winning concept," Dad said. "Something hip, something happening, something startling yet inevitable. What's the latest trend in L.A. today?"

"Mountain biking!" I exclaimed. "Everyone's doing it, even movie stars and rock musicians."

"A mountain biking restaurant?" Mom said uncertainly. "What would we serve? Fried rattlesnake?"

Dad laughed. "No, this restaurant has to be trendy, yet timeless. Unique, yet universal. Something that captures the spirit of the nineties."

"Buh-boo," Julia announced, gazing up into my father's face. "Want buh-boo."

Mom and Dad looked at each other and their eyes lit up. "Babies!" Mom exclaimed.

"Babies?" I repeated with disgust. "What are you talking about?"

"All the young actors and entertainment executives are starting families," Dad said. "And the whole country is talking about family values." He sat down beside my mother. "Sandy, I think we're on to something. We can divide the restaurant into two sections—one for adults, the other for their babies and toddlers."

"While the parents eat a quiet meal in the adult room, the babies will be served gourmet baby food," Mom continued. She smiled happily. "Ooh, think of the possibilities! I can't wait to start experimenting."

"Have you guys gone nuts?" I cried. "Taking care of one toddler is bad enough. Why in the world would you want to deal with a whole restaurant full of babies?"

"But we won't be doing it alone," Dad pointed out. "Mom will be in the kitchen, I'll be greeting and seating the customers. Then we'll have waiters, of course, and maybe some entertainment for the babies—clowns, magicians, that sort of thing." He turned to Mom. "What else do babies like?"

"Big kids," she answered. "I mean, look at Julia. She adores older children, especially Puck."

"That's perfect!" Dad exclaimed. "School's almost out. Puck will be free to help out in the dining room."

"Help out?" I cried. "Doing what?"

"Buh-boo!" Julia whined, padding over to me and drooling on my sneakers. "Want buh-boo, Uck!"

"Pretty much what you do at home," Mom said. "You can feed the baby customers and clean up after them." She turned to Julia. "What do you think, Miss Julie? Is this restaurant going to be a hit or what?"

"Hit!" Julia squealed. Then she hauled off and slugged me right in the kneecap.

Chapter
2

"No!" I shouted. "No, no, no! It's bad enough you expect me to spend half my life taking care of my pain-in-the-butt sister. No way am I going to baby-sit a roomful of slobbering, pint-sized strangers!"

"But, Puck—" Mom began.

"I said no!" I jumped up and headed for the door. "I'm going over to Jackson's. I hope you come to your senses by the time I get back. This baby restaurant idea is totally lame."

I wheeled my mountain bike off the back deck, peeled the last glob of Play-Doh from the chain, and hopped on. Soon I was coasting down the winding dirt trail that led into the canyon behind my house. I could have used the street, of course—Jackson only lives a couple of blocks away—but what fun would that have been? Instead I bounced over a few boulders, swerved between a couple of oak trees, then powered my way up the steep hill to Jackson Duprey's place.

Like our house, the Dupreys' house sits on the edge of a canyon and has a great view of the Hollywood Hills, provided the L.A. smog isn't too bad, of course. But that's where the similarities end. While our house is clean and uncluttered, with white walls and hardwood floors, Jackson's house is exploding with mismatched furniture, old newspapers, empty fast-food wrappers, and bloody corpses.

Well, not *real* corpses. You see, Jackson's parents, Zeke and Winnie, specialize in creating creepy masks and gory dummies used in horror movies and action films. For example, remember that movie about the half-human, half-robot cop—the one where the cop's arm gets blown off and blood and sparks explode everywhere? Well, that arm was created by Duprey Productions. And you know the flick about the karate expert who morphs into a dragon? Remember when the dragon steps on the bad guy's head and his eyeballs pop out? You guessed it. The head was designed and built by Jackson's mom and dad.

Anyway, Zeke and Winnie do practically all their work at home, so naturally the place is filled with jars of fake blood, packages of clay and latex, plastic brains, and almost-real-looking body parts. As for the clutter—well, Jackson's parents like to say a messy house is a lived-in house. I agree, but don't tell my parents that. They think a piece of lint on the floor is a major catastrophe.

I leaned my bike against the back of Jackson's house, took off my helmet, and climbed over the edge of the deck. "Anyone home?" I called through the sliding glass doors.

"Back here, Puck!"

I made my way through the house, stepping over books, boxes of electrical components, and dirty plates as I went. Then I turned the corner to Zeke and Winnie's workshop—and found myself face-to-face with a human-sized, lime-green praying mantis!

I let out a gasp and leaped backward, but the bug just laughed and removed its head, revealing none other than Zeke Duprey. "We're creating an army of alien bugs for a new sci-fi flick called *Creepy Crawly*," he explained. "What do you think?"

"Cool," I replied as my heart rate returned to normal. "Where's Jackson?"

"In his room, I think. Go on back."

I found Jackson sprawled across his bed, flipping through a mountain bike catalog. His cat, Benny, lay curled up on his stomach. "Hey, Puck," he said when he saw me, "what's up?"

I plopped down on the floor and told him everything. "If they think I'm going to spend my summer wiping creamed corn off a bunch of baby chins, they've got another think coming," I finished.

Jackson lifted Benny off his stomach and sat up. "Are they paying you?" he asked.

"Uh . . . gee, I don't know. We didn't discuss it."

"Look," he said, "we want new bikes, right?"

"Are you kidding? The old clunkers we're riding now barely qualify as mountain bikes." I pulled *Mountain Bike Monthly* out of my back pocket and opened it to the Cheetah 2000 ad. "Check this out. If we had a couple of these, we could really rip!"

Jackson gazed at the ad and sighed. "Killer." Then he pointed to the price—a whopping eight hundred dollars. "I don't know about you," he said, "but I'm broke. If your parents will pay me, I'll wipe creamed corn off babies' *butts*!"

I thought it over. Maybe if Table Manners hadn't folded, I could have talked my folks into getting me a new bike as an early birthday present. But now, if I wanted a Cheetah 2000, I was going to have to earn it. "If we were working together, I suppose it wouldn't be so bad," I said, trying to convince myself. "I mean, at least I'd have someone to suffer with."

"Call your parents and ask if they'll pay us," Jackson said, jumping up to search for the portable phone. He found it in the dining room, under a jumble of empty Chinese food cartons.

I called Mom and Dad, but they weren't as easy to convince as I'd hoped. They kept talking about stuff like "cash flow" and "the bottom line," and telling me how if they opened this restaurant, we all had to pitch in if we wanted it to succeed.

Then Jackson got on the phone. Within ten minutes he had convinced my parents to pay us minimum wage. In return he promised we would help feed and clean up the baby customers, plus mop the floors and scrub the restrooms every morning. "Not bad, huh?" he asked after he'd hung up. "Maybe I should be a labor negotiator when I grow up."

"Not bad?" I cried. "I didn't even want to *feed* the babies. Now you've got us mopping floors and cleaning out toilets. Am I supposed to be grateful or something?"

"Think about the money, Puck," Jackson reminded me. "Then picture yourself on a brand-new Cheetah 2000, rocketing down a dusty trail with the wind in your hair and a grin on your face."

I laughed. "You should be writing for *Mountain Bike Monthly.*"

"Someday we're going to be on the cover of *Mountain Bike Monthly,*" he said confidently.

"Yeah, but first we've got to survive this summer," I pointed out.

My parents spent the next two weeks making sure their baby restaurant concept was a sound one. First, they studied the upscale baby-oriented businesses around L.A.—stores that sold stuff like handmade baby furniture and imported baby clothing—and learned that most of them were making money hand over fist. In fact, there were more of them opening all the time.

Next, they did some marketing surveys, which means they stood around in the parking lots of exclusive day-care centers and preschools, asking parents what they thought about the idea of a gourmet restaurant for babies. People got so excited, they were practically begging my mom and dad to reserve them a table on opening night.

After that, Mom and Dad were more gung-ho than ever. Before you could say "finger food," Dad had rented a storefront on Hill Street in downtown L.A. and hired an interior designer to decorate it. Meanwhile, Mom was busy creating the menu. The adult dishes were a snap—after all, my mother's been whipping up award-winning dishes for years. But the kid stuff . . . well, that was going to be more of a challenge.

That's where Julia—and Jackson and I—came in. Mom decided that all the entrees on the children's menu had to be "kid-tested." And what better kid to test them than my very own baby sister?

"This is a restaurant for the diaper crowd?" Jackson asked as we drove up to a brick storefront. A workman was up on a ladder, painting the words *BABY BISTRO* across the front window. "It looks more like a movie-star hangout."

"This isn't a fast-food joint, you know," my mom replied. "We want the outside of the restaurant to be tasteful and subdued. But wait until you see the baby room. I think you'll like it." She grinned down at Julia, who was toddling beside her, dragging Loola by the hair. "Especially you."

We walked inside and looked around. Dad was on the adult side, supervising some workmen as they hung big abstract paintings on the exposed brick walls. The room,

with its skylight in the ceiling, cranberry-colored
and dark wood tables and chairs, looked pretty much
all the other places my mother and father had work
over the years. It was comfortable and attractive, but not
unusual.

But the kid side—now that was something else! The
walls were covered with murals of happy animals eating,
the floor was painted with green and purple swirls, and
cheerful mobiles dangled from the ceiling. There were ten
brightly colored tables, each with a built-in crayon holder
and a plastic animal as a centerpiece. To top it all off, an
overflowing toy box filled one of the room's four corners.

"Ooh!" Julia squealed when she walked in.

Mom beamed. "Take a seat," she said. "Mommy's going
to make you something to eat."

"Buh-boo?" Julia asked hopefully.

"Even better," Mom promised, hurrying off to the
kitchen.

Julia picked a red table with an alligator on it. Jackson
helped her into the fancy wooden high chair and I tied a
Baby Bistro bib around her neck. Julia grabbed a green
crayon from the crayon holder and began to scribble on the
tray of the high chair.

"No!" I cried, frantically looking around for a piece of
paper.

"Relax," Dad said, appearing at the door. "Everything is
washable—the table, the high chairs, even the walls. We're
going to give you boys a roll of paper towels and a bottle of
spray cleaner to carry in your aprons. After each baby
leaves, you just wash away the mess."

Julia finished scribbling and tossed her crayon over her
shoulder. The minute it hit the floor, she wanted it back.
"Gimme!" she whined, twisting around in her high chair.

"Well, what are you waiting for?" Dad asked. "Get her the crayon."

I frowned. "What am I, her slave?"

"For the time being, yes," Dad replied. "I want you guys to think of this afternoon as a sort of dress rehearsal. Mom is going to cook and you're going to serve Julia just as if she were a real customer."

Reluctantly, Jackson knelt down and picked up the crayon. "Here, Julia," he said.

She grabbed it from him and flung it across the room. "Gimme!" she demanded.

Dad laughed. "Good luck, boys," he said, heading for the kitchen. "And don't forget our motto: At Baby Bistro, your baby is our boss."

Jackson and I looked at each other and rolled our eyes. At that moment Mom burst through the kitchen's double doors with a platter in her hands. On it was a fish molded out of tuna salad, with scales made out of carrot slices. It was swimming in an ocean of sprouts and raisins. "Here, Miss Julie," she said, placing the dish in front of my sister. "I call this dish Swim, Little Fishie. Tell me what you think."

"Fishie!" Julia exclaimed with delight. She shoved her hand into the fish and then stuck her fingers into her mouth. But as soon as the tuna salad touched her lips, her smile faded. "Blech!" she shrieked, opening her mouth and sticking out her tongue. The tuna fell out and landed in a wet ball on the table.

"Uh-oh," Mom muttered. "See if you can coax a couple of raisins into her. I'll try another dish."

"Look, Julia," I said, kneeling beside my sister. "Raisins. Your favorite."

Julia responded by grabbing a handful of sprouts and sticking them in her hair. Then she shoved her hands into the tuna salad and began squishing it between her fingers like Play-Doh.

"Oh, gross!" Jackson cried. He reached for a napkin, but she clutched his arm, smearing tuna across it.

"Buh-boo?" she asked hopefully.

"What's she talking about?" Jackson asked, wiping off his arm.

"Buh-boo means bottle," I explained. "She wants a bottle."

"Don't worry," Mom announced, bustling out of the kitchen again. "I've got some dishes here that are guaranteed to make Julia forget her bottle."

She deposited three plates on the table. One was a skyscraper built out of peanut butter-filled celery sticks, the second was a banana "submarine" sailing through creamed-spinach "seaweed," and the last was an American flag made out of red and white bread sticks, blueberries, and cottage cheese.

"Ooh!" Julia squealed happily. She snatched a celery stick from the skyscraper's foundation, which sent the entire structure toppling onto the table.

"What a mess!" I moaned, but Mom was too busy watching Julia lick the peanut butter out of the celery sticks to notice.

"She likes it," she said happily. Then she turned to us. "Clean up the tuna and see if you can encourage her to eat the other stuff. And remember to keep her face clean. Our patrons won't be happy if they walk in here and find their kids covered with slop."

I looked at Julia. She had tuna on her cheeks, sprouts in her hair, and peanut butter on her hands. While I tried to wipe her face, she twisted in her seat and cried, "Noooo," so pathetically you would have thought I was scrubbing her skin off.

"What's wrong with her?" Jackson asked with alarm.

"She doesn't like to be cleaned up," I said. "According to this child-rearing book we have at home, all toddlers hate it."

Jackson let out a groan. "Man, I had no idea babies were so much work. I just figured—hey!"

Julia had grabbed a purple crayon and shoved it into the banana submarine. Now she lifted the banana into the air and waved it like a flag. Naturally it broke in two and fell to the floor. Julia stretched out her arm. "Gimme!"

"You can't eat it now," I said. "It's dirty."

"Want nana!" she whined. "Want nana!"

"How about a bread stick?" I suggested, handing her one.

"No!" she cried, batting it away.

"Try some creamed spinach," Jackson suggested, offering her a spoonful.

She swatted at the spoon, which sent the spinach flying. It landed with a plop on Jackson's cheek. "Yuck!" he wailed.

I started to laugh, but stopped when Julia shoved the plate containing the collapsed celery-stick skyscraper off the table. It clattered to the floor, throwing wads of peanut butter everywhere.

"I give up!" I shouted. "This is a disaster!"

"How will we manage when we have ten babies to keep happy?" Jackson asked anxiously.

"We won't," I said. "It's not humanly possible to keep ten babies happy. It's not even possible to keep Julia happy."

"Oh, I don't know about that," Jackson said suddenly. "Look."

I looked down at Julia. She was sitting amidst the wreckage of her lunch, happily chewing on a pink crayon. "Yum," she said with a smile. "Dis good."

Chapter
3

After our dress rehearsal with Julia, things happened fast. Mom put the finishing touches on the menu, while Dad began hiring waiters for the adult room, three busboys to help Jackson and me in the baby room, and an assistant chef for the kitchen. Next, Mom and Dad put ads in all the local newspapers and magazines announcing the opening of Baby Bistro. They even rented a billboard on Sunset Boulevard. It wasn't long before people were calling the restaurant, eager to make a reservation.

"Well, at least we've got opening night booked solid," Dad said one day as he glanced over the reservation book.

Mom stood on tiptoe to look over his shoulder. "Half the names on this page are either food critics, magazine reporters, or TV news anchors," she said with surprise.

"Well, you wanted to create a buzz," I pointed out. "I think you've succeeded."

Dad grinned. "In L.A., that's half the battle. If we can convince the public that our restaurant is hot, it will be."

But Mom wasn't smiling. "People are going to expect something really incredible. I just hope we can pull it off."

Dad shrugged. "We've got the best chef, the best

maitre d', and the best big brother in all of Los Angeles. What could possibly go wrong?"

"Excuse me, excuse me," shouted a hefty man with a bald baby in his arms. "What's the delay here? We've got a reservation, you know."

It was 5:01 on opening night, and already the line of impatient parents and fussy babies stretched out Baby Bistro's front door. Dad smiled his ingratiating maitre d' smile and said, "Please be patient, sir. We'll begin seating everyone with a five o'clock reservation in just a minute."

Dad hurried to the door of the baby room, where Jackson and I were standing around feeling foolish in our matching red Baby Bistro aprons. On the front were the words *IF YOU CAN READ THE MENU, YOU'RE TOO OLD FOR BABY BISTRO*. The back said, *NO DIAPER, NO BIB, NO SERVICE*. Talk about dorky! I just hoped no one from our school showed up at the restaurant. We'd never live it down.

"Bring out one of the toy baskets," Dad called to me. "Quick!"

Mom and Dad had given us five baskets of baby toys to hand out to the kids if they got bored. I grabbed one full of rattles and hurried out to the foyer. Within minutes, the basket was empty and the restaurant was filled with the sounds of shaking rattles and giggling babies.

Dad let out a relieved sigh. He peeked into the adult room to make sure everything was ready, then called the first name. "Harper, party of three."

The hefty man and his wife followed Dad into the baby room, where Julia was toddling around in a party dress, cheerfully pulling silverware off the tables. According to Mom and Dad, having Julia there would make the other babies feel welcome. Yeah, right, if she didn't demolish the place first.

Dad slipped the bald baby (I couldn't tell if it was a boy or a girl) into a high chair, and the parents ordered a Little Red Wagon (red grapes, plums, cherries, and cubes of watermelon molded into the shape of a wagon, with cottage cheese in the middle). One of the busboys took the order to Mom and her assistant, Jean-Michel, in the kitchen. Dad stuck a name tag on the baby (Terry, which didn't tell me if it was male or female), then led the parents to the adult room to order their own dinner.

The instant Terry's parents left, he (she?) burst into tears. "Don't cry, Terry," I said. "Mommy and Daddy will be back soon." I offered the kid a crayon, which only seemed to make him (her?) sob harder.

Julia walked over to investigate. "Baby cry," she pointed out. Thanks, sis. I never would have figured that out.

"I'll get something from the toy box," Jackson offered, jogging across the room.

By the time he returned with a jack-in-the-box, Dad was seating the next baby. The parents looked at Terry and frowned, obviously wondering whether they dared to leave their own little darling in our care.

Dad shot us a look that clearly said, "Shut that baby up!" I wound up the jack-in-the-box while Jackson hurried over to help Dad with the new kid. *Sproing!* The puppet popped up, but instead of laughing, Terry let out a shriek and sobbed harder.

"Food!" Dad hissed as he passed me with the second set of parents. "Get him a bread stick or something."

I ran into the kitchen. Mom and Jean-Michel were slicing, dicing, frying, and flambéing at top speed. "How's it going out there?" Mom asked as she dropped a handful of minced onions into a frying pan.

"Oh, just fine," I lied. No reason to raise her stress level unnecessarily. "Can I have some bread sticks?"

Jean-Michel grabbed a bag and tossed it to me. I hurried back into the dining room. Three more babies had been seated, and Dad was leading another two families in. I jogged over to Terry and stuck a bread stick in his (her?) mouth. Success! The kid stopped crying and started munching.

I gave a cheer, but it had barely left my lips before I heard a crash and a loud shriek. I spun around to see Julia lying under a chair that she'd apparently pulled on top of herself.

"Why is that child running around unsupervised?" a frowning mother asked.

"That's my daughter," Dad explained, laughing nervously as he pulled the chair off Julia. "She's just . . . uh, exploring, that's all."

"Well, I certainly hope my little boy isn't going to be allowed to wander off like that," the woman said. She looked around the room suspiciously. "Has this restaurant been baby-proofed?"

"Absolutely," Dad answered. "We had a child-safety expert come in and check out every inch of it. Now, if you'll follow me to the adult room . . ."

Reluctantly, the woman allowed Dad to lead her away. As they passed, I whispered, "When does the entertainment start?"

"Any minute now," he said over his shoulder. "We've got two clowns and a magician scheduled to show up at five-thirty."

I ran over to Jackson to give him the good news. He was attempting to tie a bib around the neck of a struggling toddler. "I'm tempted to just strangle her," he growled through clenched teeth.

"Shh," I hissed. "If some parent overhears you, we'll be in deep doo-doo." I handed the kid a bread stick. She laid it on the table and began pounding it into dust with her fist.

A moment later, the busboys brought the first plates of food out of the kitchen. I ran over to feed Terry his (her?) Little Red Wagon. Meanwhile, Dad was seating the last of the ten babies. "Keep up the good work," he said, patting my back as he hurried past.

I was feeding Terry a chunk of watermelon when a white-haired magician in a top hat and tails arrived and began setting up his props at the front of the room. By the time he was finished, all ten babies had their food in front of them. Fortunately, six of them were toddlers who could feed themselves. That left four babies who needed to be fed. Jackson and I scooped creamed spinach and mashed banana into two tiny mouths apiece, stopping occasionally to wipe dried food from a toddler's face.

I was extracting a crayon stub from a toddler's mouth when the magician clapped his hands and announced, "Good evening, and welcome to Baby Bistro! I am the Amazing Artemis, magician extraordinaire!" All ten babies stopped eating and stared at the magician, who snapped his fingers and produced a huge puff of black smoke.

Terry, who was sitting closest to the magician, started to cough. A toddler named Laurel burst into tears. The Amazing Artemis didn't seem to notice. He took off his hat, shouted, "Abracadabra!" and pulled out a fluffy white rabbit.

"Bunny!" Julia squealed, toddling forward. "Me pet bunny!"

The other toddlers stretched out their arms and joined in. "Pet bunny! Pet bunny!"

Okay, I figured, the guy will walk around the room and

let the kids pet the bunny. But no, he whisked the rabbit under the table and pulled out a deck of cards. Naturally, none of the kids had the slightest interest in card tricks. All they cared about was that bunny. Two or three of them began to sob pitifully.

As Jackson and I rushed over to silence them with food, the Amazing Artemis growled, "Get lost, kid!"

I spun around to see Julia crawling under the magician's table. "Hi, bunny!" she exclaimed, pulling out the cage containing the wide-eyed rabbit.

"Hey, leave the props alone!" Artemis ordered, reaching across the table to grab the bars of the cage. He pulled. Julia set her jaw and pulled back.

"Julia," I begged, rushing forward to stop her, "let's sit down and watch the nice magician. Please?"

Julia responded by switching into tantrum mode—she stiffened her body, threw back her head, and screamed bloody murder. Meanwhile, two other toddlers had escaped from their booster seats and were making their way toward the rabbit.

"That's it!" the magician shouted, throwing up his hands. "The Amazing Artemis cannot perform for such a thankless audience. I quit!" He looked down his nose at me. "Where is the owner of this establishment?"

"Uh, through those doors," I said, pointing toward the foyer.

Artemis wrenched his rabbit cage out of Julia's hands and stomped off to find my father. Jackson and I stared at each other, stunned. The babies were crying, food was flying, and Julia was still screaming about that stupid bunny.

An instant later, two clowns burst through the kitchen doors, nearly knocking over one of the busboys. They ran through the room, honking rubber horns. One of them stopped in front of a baby named Ariel and shot her with a water-squirting flower. The poor kid burst into tears. Who could blame her? With their white faces, purple hair, and raucous laughs, those clowns were so grotesque they gave *me* the creeps.

"What in heaven's name is going on in here?" a high-pitched voice demanded.

We looked up to see a plump, dark-haired woman standing at the entrance to the baby room with a look of horror on her face. She rushed over to Ariel and whisked her out of the high chair. "Oh, sweetie, are you all right?" she cooed.

Before I could think of something reassuring to say, Dad ran into the room. "What happened?" he asked me.

"Everything's out of control," I told him. "The babies hated the magician, and the clowns scared the diapers off them."

Dad sprang into action. He grabbed one of the clowns by the back of his baggy pants and said, "You're fired." He pulled some twenty dollar bills out of his pocket. "Here's your pay. Now, get lost!"

The shocked clowns took the money and walked out. Dad leaned down to whisper in my ear. "That woman's a food critic for the *Los Angeles Times*. If she leaves here mad, we're sunk. I want you and Jackson to do whatever it takes to make the babies happy. Got it? Whatever it takes."

Dad ran after the critic, who was heading for the door. I watched them go, my heart sinking. I had nodded confidently when Dad said to do whatever it took to make the babies happy, but the truth was, I had absolutely no idea how to begin. Should I feed them? We'd already tried that. Entertain them? What could Jackson and I do that a magician and two clowns couldn't?

I looked over at Julia, who was sitting on the floor hugging Loola. What did Mom and Dad do when she needed comforting? I turned to Jackson, who was standing in the middle of the room, watching helplessly as the babies sobbed, screamed, and flung their food in the air. "Sing!" I shouted to him.

"What?"

"Sing!" I launched into an off-key version of "The Itsy-Bitsy Spider." Jackson joined in, hesitantly at first, then louder.

The babies looked slightly interested, but not exactly enthralled. I switched to "Great Green Gobs of Greasy, Grimy Gopher Guts." When I got to the line "and I forgot my spoon," I grabbed a spoon from the nearest table and pretended to loudly slurp down some gopher guts.

Terry laughed. A couple of other toddlers stopped crying. Jackson gave me the thumbs-up sign. "It's working. Don't stop."

"I can't think of any other gross-out songs," I said with dismay.

"Well, do *something*," he insisted.

Suddenly I remembered a trick I'd used once to make Julia laugh. I grabbed a pacifier from the table of a toddler named Rory and pretended to swallow it. Actually, I used my tongue to hide it against the inside of my cheek. "Where'd it go?" I asked the kids. Then I opened my mouth and pretended to retch. The pacifier flew out onto the floor.

Rory laughed. Julia toddled over and said, "Again, Uck!"

So I did it again. And again. The kids were in hysterics. Meanwhile, Jackson ran around the room, cleaning up the babies and slipping a few bites of food into their mouths.

It was right about then that Dad returned with the food critic and her daughter. When he saw that the kids were happy and clean, his face lit up like the lights on the Sunset Strip. The critic looked around thoughtfully. "Hmm," she said, returning her baby to her high chair, "perhaps I was a bit hasty in my judgment of this place."

Dad spoke some encouraging words to her, then hurried over to my side. "What did you do?" he asked, obviously impressed.

When I told him, his smile faded. "That's disgusting."

"Yeah, but it worked."

He thought it over. "Okay, go for it. Just try not to do anything too obnoxious while a parent is in the room."

Jackson and I spent the rest of the evening juggling baby bottles, standing on our hands, singing stupid songs, pretending to take out our eyeballs and wash them, and any other ridiculous thing we could think of. The kids loved it. Between five and nine o'clock, we fed, cleaned, and entertained forty babies, and every one of them left happy. They didn't even complain when we wiped their faces.

"We really owe you guys," Dad said after the last well-fed baby had left. "You saved us from becoming the only restaurant in L.A. to close after one night."

"How about a raise?" Jackson asked immediately.

"Sorry, not until we start making some money ourselves," Mom replied, taking off her chef's hat and shaking out her hair. "But we'll make a deal. If you continue entertaining the babies, you won't have to mop the floors and clean the bathrooms."

"Forget it," I said. "It's bad enough feeding and wiping the little beasts. If I have to sing 'Greasy, Grimy Gopher Guts' one more time, I'll scream."

"Oh, come on," Jackson whispered, taking me aside. "Entertaining babies isn't so bad. Besides, once we make ourselves indispensable, we'll have your folks right where we want them. Either we get paid enough to buy new mountain bikes by the middle of August, or we walk."

Man, what a negotiator! "I'm just glad you're on my side," I said. I turned to Mom and Dad. "Okay, we'll do it. All I ask is one thing."

"What's that?" Dad wondered.

"Take me to the Burger Barn and buy me a Triple-Mondo-Mega Cheeseburger. I'm starving!"

Dad laughed and shook his head. "And to think you're the son of a gourmet chef." He scooped up Julia, who had fallen asleep in the toy box. "Come on, guys, let's eat."

Chapter
4

"There, that should do it," Jackson said, placing two heavy rocks on the base of the orange traffic cone that was sitting on our deck. He stood up and turned to me. "Well, what do you think?"

I walked around the contraption we had just constructed, checking it out. It consisted of the traffic cone with a broom handle sticking through the hole in the top. Attached to the handle was a free-spinning bicycle tire, and buckled to the tire were Pepperoni's leash and one of Dad's belts.

"Brilliant," I said with satisfaction. "Now let's try it out. You catch Pepperoni and I'll find Julia."

It was a Saturday afternoon, two weeks after Baby Bistro had opened. In the intervening weeks, the restaurant had received nothing but glowing reviews, including one in *American Gourmet* that called it "an introduction to fine dining for young Americans, disguised as an evening of fun and frolic." Since then, the phone had been ringing off the hook with people wanting reservations. TV and movie stars, rock musicians, entertainment executives—they all wanted to eat at Baby Bistro. If they didn't have kids of their own, they borrowed some. The important thing was to be seen walking through the restaurant's front door.

I was thrilled about my parents' success, of course, and plenty relieved that we weren't going to be forced to sell our house and live in a cardboard box under a freeway overpass. What didn't thrill me was those darned babies. Imagine spending every night of the week (except Mondays, when we were closed) feeding, cleaning, and entertaining forty babies. If I had to pretend to retch up a pacifier one more time, I swear I was going to lose my mind.

On top of that, my parents had the nerve to make me give up what little free time I had to baby-sit Julia. Like now, for example. Mom and Dad were at the farmers' market buying fruits and vegetables for the restaurant, and I was stuck at home playing nursemaid to my little sister. Thank goodness Jackson had come over and helped me rig up the mechanical baby-sitter on the deck. I just hoped it would work.

"Julia!" I called, walking through the house. "Julia, where are you?"

I found her in the kitchen with her head inside the open refrigerator, happily munching on a stick of butter. With a sigh, I wrenched the butter from her fist, wiped her face on a towel, and dragged her out to the deck. Jackson was there, slipping Pepperoni's collar around his neck. Before Julia could protest, I whisked her over to the contraption and strapped Dad's belt around her chest, just under her arms.

"No!" she shrieked, wiggling wildly.

But then she spotted Pepperoni, just two feet in front of her. "Roni!" she squealed, grabbing for his tail. Naturally, Pepperoni tried to run away, but since he was tied to the bicycle wheel, all he could do was trot in a circle. Julia padded after him. The wheel turned, Pepperoni barked, and Julia lunged for his tail, which was always just inches out of reach. Around and around they went, like a couple of mice in a wheel.

I slapped Jackson a high five. "Works like a charm," I said, stretching out on a lounge chair.

"This is the life," he agreed, flopping down on the hammock. "Now, what's this idea you wanted to talk to me about?"

"Let's construct a mountain bike course at the bottom of the canyon. We can have jumps and water hazards and everything."

"Cool," Jackson said thoughtfully. "But how do we create a water hazard in the middle of summer? It's dry as a bone down there."

"I already thought of that. We hook up a hose to our washing machine and run the waste water down the hillside to the hazards."

"Awesome. We can even set up an obstacle course with boulders, and build dirt ramps, and—"

The sound of the front door opening made my heart leap into my throat. "They're back!" I gasped, jumping out of the lounge chair. "Quick, unbuckle Jul—"

Too late. Mom and Dad opened the door to the deck and stopped short. "What's going on out here?" Mom demanded.

"We're, uh, giving Julia and Pepperoni some exercise," I said. "See, they love it."

As if on cue, Julia flung herself at Pepperoni's tail. The two of them trotted around the wheel, laughing and barking. Mom smiled in spite of herself. "They really do look cute. Brad, go get the video camera."

"Okay, okay, but first tell Puck and Jackson the big news."

"The farmers' market didn't have everything we wanted," Mom said, "so we left and stopped by the restaurant on the way home to check our messages. You'll never guess who made a reservation."

"Shaquille O'Neal?" I suggested.

"Arnold Schwarzenegger?" Jackson asked.

"No, no, no," Dad said. "Even better. Our first celebrity baby."

"A baby?" I said, wrinkling my nose. "Who?"

"Sissy Rae Comstock!" Mom proclaimed.

"Who the heck is she?" Jackson asked.

"Oh, I'm sure you've seen her," Dad said. "She's the little girl who does the Puff 'N' Soft Toilet Tissue commercial on TV."

"You mean that pudgy little twerp with the curly red hair?" Jackson asked.

"Her?" I cried. "Yuck! She's obnoxious!"

"I think she's adorable," Mom insisted. "I love it when she walks away from the camera, trailing that roll of toilet paper behind her, then looks over her shoulder and says, 'Time to go!'"

"Oh, Mom, please!" I moaned. "Don't make me barf."

"Hey, don't make fun of Sissy Rae," Dad scolded. "Since those ads have started airing, she's become a huge star. The Puff 'N' Soft people have signed her to do a whole series of commercials for them, and according to what I read in the newspaper, she's already rich."

"She must be," Mom remarked. "Her mother has reserved the entire restaurant this Wednesday night just for Sissy Rae."

Jackson turned to me, a look of misery on his face. "And just think, we get to feed her, and entertain her, and—"

"And treat her nicely," Dad broke in. "You got that, boys? Sissy Rae is a celebrity, and if she doesn't leave the Baby Bistro with a full stomach and a smile on her face,

Hollywood is going to hear about it. And that would be very bad for us."

What could I say? I couldn't let Mom and Dad down. But a whole evening of sucking up to Sissy Rae Comstock? The kid just had to be a spoiled brat, I was sure of it. I wouldn't be surprised if she made Julia look like a little angel in comparison.

Still, I couldn't really complain. If Mom and Dad hadn't come home all excited about Sissy Rae, they undoubtedly would have nailed me for strapping Julia and Pepperoni to the bicycle wheel. I figured I'd better humor them.

"We'll treat her like a princess," I promised.

Pepperoni picked that moment to lift his leg and pee on the traffic cone.

"Oh, Pepperoni!" I cried. "Bad dog!"

But Julia just grinned as if it was the most entertaining thing she'd ever seen. Then she turned to us and announced in her best Sissy Rae voice, "Time to go!"

Mom and Dad spent the next four days reading every magazine article about Sissy Rae they could get their hands on. They learned she was two-and-a-half years old and an only child. She and her mother, Violet (who was also her manager), had moved to Hollywood from Iowa a mere six months ago. Since then, Sissy Rae's career had taken off. Besides the series of Puff 'N' Soft commercials, there was talk of a Sissy Rae TV show, maybe even a movie. In short, the kid was hot.

By Wednesday night, I'd learned more about Sissy Rae Comstock than I ever wanted to know. But as soon as Dad walked into the baby room with Sissy Rae, her mother, and an unknown man, I found out a lot more.

"Sissy Rae," Dad said, "I'd like you to meet Puck and

Jackson. They'll be feeding you dinner tonight."

"How old are these kids?" Sissy Rae's mother broke in, patting her puffy blond hair. She was a plump woman, wearing too-tight white leather pants, a low-cut red blouse, and enough makeup to supply all the clowns in the circus. "Are they licensed day-care providers?"

"Sissy Rae is a star, you know," growled her companion, a balding man with a beer belly, who was wearing an expensive suit and smoking a fat cigar. "We're not going to leave her with just anybody."

"Of course not, Mr. Comstock," Dad said in a sugary voice.

"I'm not Mr. Comstock," the man shot back. "I'm Irving Steinwald, and in case you've been living in a cave, I'm the one who produced Sissy Rae's Puff 'N' Soft commercial."

"Excuse me, Mr. Steinwald," Dad said, forcing himself to smile. "I just didn't recognize you right away. Believe me, you don't have to worry about Puck and Jackson. They're experienced baby-sitters who have fed, cleaned, and entertained literally hundreds of babies since our restaurant opened. I guarantee your little angel will be in good hands with them."

"Let's hope so," Violet Comstock said haughtily. She picked up a menu from a nearby table and looked it over. "This will never do. Sissy Rae is allergic to bananas, peanut butter, tomatoes—oh, yes, and all forms of milk and wheat."

If I had been in charge, right about then I would have told Violet and her pushy boyfriend to take a hike. But my father is a professional. "Just make me a list of all the foods Sissy Rae is allergic to," he said pleasantly. "I'm sure our chef can prepare something suitable for your daughter."

"Yes, but will she like it?" Violet asked. "My Sissy Rae is a very picky eater."

"Don't you worry," Dad said, ushering Violet and Irving toward the adult room. "Puck and Jackson will take care of everything."

We will? I looked down at Sissy Rae, who was standing there in a flouncy pink dress and black patent-leather shoes, watching her mother walk away. It was the first time I'd really looked at her since she arrived, and what I saw surprised me. I'd expected a flirty little chatterbox, the kind of girl who knows she's cute and expects everyone else to think so, too. But Sissy Rae seemed quiet and subdued. Her arms hung at her sides, and her eyes were blank. To tell you the truth, she looked kind of depressed.

"Come on, Sissy Rae," I said, reaching down to take her hand, "let's have some fun."

She looked up at me forlornly, then turned to gaze out the window at the street. "Daddy coming?" she asked.

"Uh, I don't know," Jackson said. "Hey, Sissy Rae, what's your favorite food?"

Sissy Rae didn't answer. She toddled slowly toward the toy box, then stood there staring at the toys.

"Go ahead," I said. "You can play with anything you want."

Sissy Rae hesitated, then reached for a brightly colored music box. I showed her how to turn the handle. When the music began, her eyes grew wide with wonder.

"What doing, Uck?" a small voice asked.

I looked over my shoulder to see Julia walking out of the kitchen, where she'd been taking a nap. "Hey, Julia, this is Sissy Rae," I said. "Can you say hi?"

When Sissy Rae saw Julia, her face lit up. "Music box," she said, holding it up.

"Me dance," Julia cooed happily. She began to sway and spin, hugging her baby doll, Loola, to her chest. Soon Sissy

Rae joined in. The two of them looked so funny—Julia with her wrinkled playsuit and messy hair, Sissy Rae with her party dress and perfect red curls—shaking like two bowls of Jell-O.

Suddenly the door to the baby room flew open and Violet Comstock walked in. "What is going on?" she snapped. "My daughter came here to eat, not to pick up germs from a bunch of grubby toys that who-knows-how-many other children have touched."

"The toys are cleaned every night," I said. "Besides, she's having fun."

Violet was unimpressed. "Who is this child?" she asked, pointing at Julia. "I thought I reserved the entire restaurant."

"That's my sister," I answered. "She likes to play with the customers."

"I don't allow Sissy Rae to play with babies," Violet said. "It doesn't challenge her brain."

What was she talking about? Julia was only six months younger than Sissy Rae. Besides, what did it matter, as long as they were happy? But then I thought about what Dad would do in this situation and forced myself to smile. "Whatever you say, Mrs. Comstock."

I picked Julia up and carried her toward the kitchen. Naturally, she burst out crying. As soon as Sissy Rae realized her playmate was leaving, she began sobbing, too.

"My daughter is hungry," Violet said with a frown. "Where's her dinner?"

Like the answer to a prayer, Mom walked out of the kitchen at that very moment, carrying a platter of food arranged in the shape of a clown. She set it on one of the tables and turned to Violet. "Your dinner is ready, too, Mrs. Comstock. May I escort you to the adult room?"

Violet allowed Mom to lead her away. I gave Julia to Jean-Michel and hurried back into the baby room. Jackson had lifted Sissy Rae into a high chair and was offering her a slice of mango. She stuck out her lower lip and shook her head. He held out a raisin. She shouted "No!" then looked out the window again. "Daddy coming?" she asked hopefully.

"I bet your daddy would want you to eat something," I said. I picked up the salt and pepper shakers and began to juggle them. Sissy Rae managed a tiny smile.

Jackson grabbed a cracker, tossed it into the air, and caught it in his mouth. Sissy Rae's smile grew a little wider. "Come on, Sissy Rae," he urged, holding out a cracker, "now *you* try one."

Sissy Rae's smile disappeared and her lower lip popped out again. "No," she said grumpily.

Just then, Violet marched back into the room. My heart sank as she gazed at the untouched food. "What is wrong with you people?" she demanded. "Those crackers have butter in them. I *told* you Sissy Rae is allergic to dairy products." She turned on her heel and marched into the kitchen.

I ran to the door and peeked in. "These are all-natural crackers," Mom was saying. "We make them ourselves. They have no butter in them, just vegetable oil."

Violet nibbled the edge of the cracker. "I don't believe it. I can taste the butter."

"Madame, I baked zose crackers myself," Jean-Michel said in his thick French accent. "Zey do not contain butter."

"Who are you?" Violet asked. "The busboy?"

"Busboy!" Jean-Michel gasped. "I am ze assistant chef."

"Well, then, you ought to know what's in the food you serve."

Jean-Michel stared at Violet, his dark eyes flashing. "Are you calling me a liar?"

"Jean-Michel, calm down," Mom pleaded. "Mrs. Comstock, please go back to your table. We'll take good care of your daughter."

"All right, but I do hope you'll get some better help here in the future. At least find someone who can speak English."

"Enough!" Jean-Michel cried, throwing up his hands. "I am an artist. I have cooked for royalty, for movie stars, for opera singers. I will not be insulted by ze mother of some flash-in-ze-pan child star."

"Flash in the pan!" Violet gasped. "Sissy Rae is a superstar. You apologize this instant or I'll have you fired."

"Do not bother," Jean-Michel shot back. "I quit!" With that, he took off his apron, flung it on the floor, and stomped out the back door.

Mom looked like she was about to have a nervous breakdown. She gazed at Violet, then at the door that Jean-Michel had walked through, then back at Violet. "Please, Mrs. Comstock," she said at last, her voice stiff and strained, "I can't cook with customers in the kitchen. If you sit down, I promise you Sissy Rae will get a good dinner."

I jumped out of the way as Violet let out a "hurrumph" and walked back through the swinging doors into the baby room. She shot me a withering look, then turned and strode off to the adult room.

I ran back to Sissy Rae's table, where Jackson was singing "On Top of Spaghetti" and urging her to try a celery stick. "We have to get some food into her—and fast," I said. I picked up a grape and held it out to her. She gazed at it, unmoved. In desperation, I dipped the grape into a blob of ketchup on the clown's french-fry hair.

Sissy Rae watched with interest. Then, to my amazement, she opened her mouth. I held my breath and

44

placed the ketchup-covered grape on her tongue. She bit down on it—and smiled.

"She likes it!" Jackson exclaimed.

"Quick, give her some more!"

We spent the next ten minutes feeding Sissy Rae ketchup-covered grapes. Then we moved on to other weird combinations, like olives sprinkled with pepper, and crackers covered with jelly and mustard. She loved it all, but her favorite food, hands down, was spinach with chocolate sauce.

When Dad came in a few minutes later to check on things, he found Sissy Rae happily munching away. "Oh, thank heavens," he said with a relieved sigh. "You boys are geniuses."

Violet and Irving showed up a few minutes later. By that time, Sissy Rae had eaten her fill, been wiped off, and was giggling with delight as Jackson and I played leapfrog around her table.

"Well, the kid looks pretty happy," Irving said. He turned to Dad. "My compliments to the chef. That chocolate pecan pie was out of this world."

"Thank you very much," Dad said, beaming. "I do hope you'll come back to Baby Bistro again."

Believe it or not, Violet smiled. It was as if the last two hours hadn't even happened. "Oh, you can count on it," she said.

I stifled a groan. I'm not sure which was worse—having Violet and Irving bad-mouthing our restaurant to everyone in Hollywood, or having them come back. I glanced at Jackson and rolled my eyes. He pretended to gag, and I froze, frightened Violet and Irving would notice. But the only person watching was Sissy Rae, and she thought it was funny.

She clapped her hands and nibbled on one last ketchup-covered grape. "Again!" she said with a grin.

Chapter
5

Mom and Dad were still sleeping when Jackson came over the next morning to start work on our mountain bike course. Our plan was to browse through our collection of mountain biking magazines to learn about the courses that had been used for some of the sport's most famous races, like the World Cup, the Olympic Trials, and the World Championships. Julia was occupied giving Loola a bath in the kitchen sink, so we dumped our pile of magazines on my bedroom floor and got to work.

"I didn't eat breakfast," Jackson said, grabbing a mag. "What have you got in your secret stash?"

"Junk food for breakfast?" I asked.

"Hey, around here, you've got to go for it whenever you can, right, dude?"

I had to agree. You see, my folks refuse to allow any foods in our house that contain chemicals, additives, or processed sugar. In other words, no candy bars, no cupcakes, no ice cream sandwiches. Whenever they want something sweet to eat, Mom whips up a dark chocolate mousse or a flourless hazelnut torte—good stuff, but not exactly my idea of the perfect munchie.

Fortunately, Mom and Dad don't know about my secret stash of junk food, bought with my allowance and hidden beneath a blanket on the top shelf of my closet. I jumped up and pulled down a bag of licorice, candy corn, and chocolate bars.

"Mmm, good stuff," Jackson remarked, digging in.

At the first sound of crinkling cellophane, Julia appeared at my door. We gave her a handful of candy corn to keep her quiet and went back to our magazines.

"Puck," my mom called a few minutes later, "are you awake? Come in here. Quick!"

I gulped down my chocolate bar and ran into my parents' bedroom. Mom and Dad were sitting up in bed, watching TV. "Look," my dad said, pointing at the screen.

They were watching *L.A. Your Way*, a morning news and entertainment show. ". . . at L.A.'s hottest new restaurant, Baby Bistro," the announcer was saying. "Let's take a look."

They cut to some video footage of Sissy Rae Comstock, her mother, and Irving Steinwald walking out of the restaurant.

"According to our sources," the announcer continued, "Sissy Rae, who is known as a picky eater, loved her meal. Her mother and manager, Violet Comstock, and Violet's escort, Puff 'N' Soft commercial producer Irving Steinwald, were quoted as saying, 'We'll be back!'"

A commercial came on and my mother turned off the TV. "Can you believe it?" she exclaimed. "We made the morning news!"

"Keeping Sissy Rae and her mother happy was the hardest thing I've ever done, but it was worth it," Dad said. "You can't buy this kind of publicity."

"Now do we get a raise?" Jackson asked, appearing at the door of the bedroom.

"Yes," my father said. "You boys deserve it. I'll increase your salary by fifty cents an hour."

"All right!" Jackson and I shouted, giving each other a hearty chest butt.

At that moment, Julia walked into the room, hugging my bag of junk food to her chest. "Uck share," she announced, munching on a gooey piece of licorice.

Dad grabbed the bag from her and looked inside. "What is this stuff doing in our house?" he cried. "Puck, you know we don't approve of artificial foods, especially processed sugar."

"But you let me eat Triple-Mondo-Mega Cheeseburgers," I pointed out.

"Once in a while," Dad admitted. "But it doesn't make me happy. Anyway, it isn't the candy that bothers me so much as the fact that you were eating it behind our backs." He turned to my mother. "I think this deserves a punishment, don't you, Sandy?"

But Mom wasn't listening. She was staring into space, a look of dismay on her face. "Jean-Michel quit," she muttered. "The restaurant opens in exactly eight hours and I don't have an assistant chef."

Dad slapped his forehead with the heel of his hand. "The place is booked solid," he groaned. "Do you think you can handle it by yourself?"

"Are you kidding? Jean-Michel and I together could barely keep on top of things. I was planning to ask you if we could afford to hire more help."

"Get on the phone," Dad said, handing her the portable. "Do whatever it takes to woo Jean-Michel back."

Jackson nudged me in the ribs with his elbow, then motioned toward the door. I nodded. This was our chance to sneak out without anyone noticing. Slowly, quietly, we

48

edged toward the door. I had to leave the bag of junk food behind, but it was worth it to escape without a punishment.

"Hit the trail," I whispered.

We tiptoed out to the deck, vaulted over the edge, and pedaled our bikes down into the canyon. It was a gorgeous day, warm and breezy. The birds were singing, dust was flying. I swerved left to avoid a rock, then attempted a tight cutback to the right, which made my bike's front end wobble. I tried to adjust, overcompensated, and hit the dirt.

"Stupid bike!" I growled. "I might as well be riding a tricycle!"

"Relax," Jackson said, hitting the brakes and reaching down to help me up. "We got a raise, remember? Pretty soon you'll be riding a brand-new Cheetah 2000 with an extra-roomy V-style frame to handle those tight turns."

I stood up, grinning. Who cared if we had to spend our nights sponging up baby spit? What did it matter if my little sister was a walking, talking tornado, or that my precious bag of junk food had been confiscated? Soon the Cheetah 2000 would be mine!

"Jean-Michel, please," Mom pleaded into the phone while Julia tugged at her leg, "I'll pay you whatever you want. I'll give you Sundays off. Anything. Just say you'll come back."

Mom was standing in the foyer of Baby Bistro, a loose strand of hair hanging in her eyes and a look of desperation on her face. This was the third time she'd spoken to Jean-Michel in the last eight hours, and he'd already refused her twice. Apparently he'd been thinking of quitting ever since the night Baby Bistro opened. Violet's insults had just been the last straw.

"I despise babies," Jean-Michel had told Mom. "And I

now realize I despise cooking for zem, too. If I have to create another dish in ze shape of a clown, I will lose my mind!"

Mom had spent most of the afternoon on the phone with her many restaurant friends, trying to find an assistant chef who was talented, experienced, and available immediately. So far, she'd struck out. That's why she was talking to Jean-Michel again.

"No!" I heard Jean-Michel shout on the other end of the phone. "A thousand times no. Cooking for babies is an insane idea!" Then he slammed down the receiver.

"We're sunk," she said, hanging up. "It's four-thirty and I've got the busboys in there chopping carrots for me. This is hopeless."

"Is there anything I can do?" I asked.

"Yes, you can entertain Julia. She's been crawling all over me this afternoon."

I tried to pick her up, but she went limp and slid to the floor. "Want Mommy—and buh-boo," she added for good measure.

"Mommy has to cook now," I said. "But you can watch her if you promise to be good."

"Good," Julia agreed with a nod.

We followed Mom through the baby room, where Jackson was setting the tables, and into the kitchen. The busboys, who would normally be doing Jackson's job, were lined up at the counter, chopping carrots, washing lettuce, and grinding chopped fruit in the food processor.

"No, no, no!" Mom cried, hurrying over. "You're liquefying the fruit instead of pureeing it. And look at these carrots. I need thin slices, not huge chunks." She ran her hands through her hair. "This is a disaster. A *disaster*!"

The busboys looked at her blankly. Julia picked that moment to reach up and grab a bottle from the counter. The loose top fell off, and two quarts of Mom's homemade house salad dressing splashed to the floor.

"Oh, no!" Mom wailed. "Puck, I thought I told you to keep an eye on her!"

"I'm sorry," I said. "I just . . ."

My voice trailed off as a tall, lanky man appeared at the door that led into the back alley. He had stooped shoulders, a friendly face with a long nose and droopy eyes, and short brown hair with a cowlick in the back. "Excuse me," he said in a soft Southern drawl, "I'm lookin' for a job. Can you use some kitchen help?"

Mom spun around and stared at him. "I can't believe this," she said with a laugh. "Are you an angel sent from heaven to save me from a nervous breakdown?"

"Well, I don't know about that," he replied. "I'm just Will Faraday from Hot Springs, Arkansas, but I'll do the best I can."

"Have you ever worked as an assistant chef?" Mom asked hopefully.

"No, ma'am. Back in Arkansas, I was a short-order cook. But I'm a fast learner."

Mom's hopeful look disappeared. "Well, it was a nice fantasy while it lasted." She shook her head. "I'm sorry, Mr. Faraday, but this is a gourmet restaurant. I need someone who's had experience cooking nouvelle cuisine."

At that moment the door that led to the adult room burst open and Dad rushed in. "The babies are arriving, and get this—they're all beauty pageant contestants. You know what prima donnas those kids can be. And the parents . . ." He paused and looked curiously at the tall man with the friendly smile. "Who's this?"

"Will Faraday," he said. "The new assistant chef, if things go my way." He turned to Mom. "Like I said, I'm a fast learner, and a hard worker, too. Why don't you give me a try? If it doesn't work out, I'll take my leave with no pay and no hard feelings."

Julia, who had been watching the busboys wipe up the salad dressing from the floor, turned and gazed up at Will for the first time. "Big," she announced with wonder in her voice.

Will laughed and knelt down in front of her. He gazed curiously at her left ear and asked, "Now what's that doing in there?" He reached into her ear, then opened his hand, and there in his palm was a small rubber unicorn.

Julia fell for the trick, hook, line, and sinker. She beamed and reached for the unicorn as if it were a precious diamond. Will gave it to her and she held it tight.

"You're hired—on a trial basis, that is," Mom said. "Busboys, back to the baby room. You, too, Puck. Will, I want you to toss together a large bowl of watercress, arugula, and Bibb lettuce while I make some new salad dressing."

"I don't know those fancy names," he replied, "but point 'em out to me and I'll do my best."

Dad rushed back to the foyer, and I carried Julia into the baby room. I had barely told Jackson about Will Faraday's arrival before the first babies were being seated. After that, everything was a blur. Jackson and I juggled, sang, fed, and cleaned until we were about to drop.

At one point I ran into the kitchen to grab some extra raisins. Will was arranging sprouts on a plate with one hand and tossing a paper airplane for Julia with the other. The plane did two loop-de-loops and landed at my feet.

"Lane fly!" Julia squealed, toddling over to retrieve it.

"Can you teach me to make one of those?" I asked Will. "Anything that keeps Julia busy for more than ten seconds is in big demand at my house."

"Well, sure," he replied. "Hey, is that your bicycle out in the alley?"

I nodded. "My friend, Jackson, and I ride our bikes here sometimes. They're not really street bikes though."

"They're mountain bikes, right? I once tried riding one of those things back in Arkansas. Took off down a hill and almost broke my neck," he added with a chuckle. "But it was exciting, I'll say that."

"Puck, don't you have some babies to feed?" Mom asked.

"Oh, yeah, sorry. I came in for raisins."

Will grabbed a bag of raisins and tossed it over his shoulder. It landed right in my hands. "Not bad," I said with a grin.

"Used to play high school football back in Des Moines."

"I thought you said you come from Arkansas."

"I do," Will replied. "By way of Des Moines."

"Puck, get going," Mom commanded.

But I didn't want to leave. The kitchen had a whole different feel now that Jean-Michel was gone and Will was working beside Mom. It was more relaxed, more friendly. I knew Julia could feel it, too. That's why she was there instead of playing in the baby room.

"Puck . . ." Mom warned.

"I'll teach you how to make that airplane later," Will said with a smile.

I smiled back, then took a deep breath and headed back to face the babies.

At nine o'clock the last well-fed baby left the restaurant with her parents. Jackson and I took off our aprons and strolled into the kitchen. Mom was feeding Julia a bowl of boysenberry-banana pudding while Will wiped the counter with a wet sponge. Dad arrived a moment later. I could tell

53

just by looking at him that the evening had been a success.

"We didn't receive one complaint about the food or the service all evening," he said with satisfaction. "How'd it go in here?"

"Surprisingly well," Mom said with a smile. "Will may not be a trained chef, but he knows his way around a kitchen and he's got good instincts. With a little experience, he'll make an outstanding assistant chef."

Will stopped wiping. "Does that mean I'm hired?" he asked.

Dad looked at Mom. She nodded, and I felt my face break into a grin. "Welcome to Baby Bistro," Dad said, shaking his hand.

Will was grinning, too. "Thank you, Mr. Rosen."

"Anyone want some of this leftover food?" Mom asked, peering into the pots on the stove. "I've got a little roast chicken, some spinach and chives, and lots of garlic mashed potatoes."

I wrinkled my nose. "Can't we stop at Burger Barn on the way home?"

"Uh, excuse me, but I'll take some of that food," Will broke in. "That is, if no one else wants it."

Mom looked at Jackson and me and sighed. "Go on. These boys don't appreciate my cooking."

Quickly, Will piled a plate with food, set it on the counter, and dug in. To watch him eat, you'd think he was starving.

Dad noticed it, too. "When's the last time you had a square meal, Will?" he asked.

"Three days ago, sir," he said between bites. "The day I arrived in Los Angeles." He looked at Mom and smacked his lips. "Ma'am, I may not be a food expert, but I declare this sure tastes fine."

Chapter

6

"This is jicama," Mom said, holding up a chunk of something white and applelike. "Very nice in salads, and of course toddlers like it because it's got a mild taste and they can eat it with their fingers."

Mom handed the chunk to Will and he took a bite. "Hmm, not half bad. You could make a dish for the babies in the shape of a snowman with jicama, coconut, white cheese . . ."

"What a marvelous idea!" Mom exclaimed. "Imagine a 3-D snowman made out of grated cheese and apple, with raisin eyes."

Will nodded. "And an igloo built with blocks of that jicama stuff."

"Fabulous," Mom agreed. She picked up the next object on the counter, a bowl filled with little green things. "Now, these are capers."

It was Saturday afternoon, and Jackson, Julia, and I were hanging out in the Baby Bistro kitchen while Mom taught Will about the foods she used in nouvelle cuisine. It had been a week since he first walked through our back door, and already we'd all grown to love him—Mom and Dad because he was a hard worker with good ideas, Julia because he was never too busy to tickle her or toss her into the air, and Jackson and me because he knew a million ways to entertain kids and was always willing to share them.

Take that paper airplane he made for Julia during his first night on the job. I folded one now and sat down in the doorway next to Jackson. He was hunched over a pad of paper, making sketches of our soon-to-be-constructed mountain bike course. I could still see the ketchup in the corner of his mouth from the two Triple-Mondo-Mega Cheeseburgers he had recently devoured. Mom didn't know it, but the main reason we liked to ride our bikes to work was so we could stop at Burger Barn on the way.

"Okay, so the first water hazard goes here," Jackson said, pointing to a circle with wiggly lines he had drawn on a piece of computer paper, "then three dirt moguls right—"

"No, no, this is where we put the boulders to make the serpentine," I broke in. "*Then* the moguls."

"Want dat," Julia announced, toddling up behind us and grabbing for Jackson's pencil.

I immediately launched the paper airplane across the kitchen and cried, "Go get it, Julia!"

She let out a squeal and took off after it. She'd barely gotten three feet before she became distracted by a whisk that Mom had given her to play with. I smiled as she plopped down on the floor to examine it. With luck, we had at least five minutes before she remembered the airplane, let alone us.

We had mapped out almost the entire course when Dad walked in from the baby room. "Red alert!" he exclaimed. "Violet Comstock just called. She's bringing Sissy Rae here tonight, along with her agent, Pearl Pendergast."

Will spun around, his eyes wide. "Sissy Rae?" he asked. "Here? Tonight?"

"Are you a Sissy Rae fan?" Mom asked.

"Me?" Will shrugged nonchalantly. "I wouldn't go that far. I've seen her TV commercial. She's a cute kid."

"And a pain in the butt," I added under my breath.

"Puck," Mom scolded, "hush."

But Will turned to me. "What do you mean, Puck?"

"Well, to tell you the truth, it's her mother who's the real pain," I said. "Sissy Rae is just sort of . . . well, unhappy, I guess. She pouts a lot, and she's always whining for her father."

"Isn't he around?" Will asked.

"According to the articles I've read, he left the family, and Violet and he are divorced," Dad replied. "That's all I know."

"Sissy Rae's a real picky eater," Jackson added. "But we found something she loves. Spinach with chocolate sauce."

Will laughed. "I bet I know something else she'd go for. Tonight, try feedin' her french fries with maple syrup on top."

"What makes you think she'd like that?" Mom asked. "Do you have a picky eater of your own at home?"

Will shook his head, a little sadly, I thought. "Nope, I don't have kids. French fries with syrup was one of my favorites when I was a youngster."

"You must be a picky eater yourself," Dad remarked. "How does your wife feel about that?"

"No wife either," he replied with a shrug. "Guess I just haven't found the right gal."

"Maybe we can introduce you to Violet Comstock," Jackson cracked. "She's a real sweetheart."

I snickered, but Dad frowned. "No bad-mouthing the

customers," he said sternly. "Now I would suggest you boys get into your aprons and start practicing your silly songs. With Sissy Rae and her mother here, it's bound to be a lo-o-ong night."

"Did you hear the news?" Violet asked my father as they led Sissy Rae into the baby room. "Our TV sitcom has been green-lighted by the network. We begin shooting next month."

"There's going to be all sorts of merchandising tie-ins," the woman beside her said in a gravelly voice. She was short and stocky, with leathery skin, black hair, and pointy, diamond-studded glasses that hung around her neck on a chain. "Sissy Rae dolls, Sissy Rae diapers, even a whole line of Sissy Rae clothing."

"Why, that's wonderful," Dad said, lifting Sissy Rae into her high chair.

But if Sissy Rae felt the same way, you'd never know it to look at her. She stuck out her lower lip and sighed. "Daddy coming?" she asked in a plaintive voice.

Violet ignored her. "This is Pearl Pendergast, Sissy Rae's agent," she said. "I told her what a fabulous restaurant this is. I certainly hope she won't be disappointed."

"I know you won't be, Ms. Pendergast," Dad said, smiling as he held out his arm. "May I show the two of you to the adult room?"

Violet looked back over her shoulder at Jackson and me. "Don't forget about Sissy Rae's food allergies. One bite of tomato and she breaks out in hives. And keep her away from the other kids. If she catches a cold and the taping of her first TV show has to be postponed, I'm going to hold you boys personally responsible."

Jackson smiled through clenched teeth. "What a witch!" he said under his breath.

I waved as Violet walked away. "I hope she chokes on a chicken bone," I whispered.

As soon as Violet and Pearl Pendergast were gone, Jackson hurried off to feed one of the babies, and I turned to Sissy Rae. "Remember me?" I asked. I grabbed a bread stick off the table, twirled it like a baton, then took a big, noisy bite.

Sissy Rae managed a weak smile. She gazed longingly at the other children, who were eating, rubbing food into their hair, crawling around the floor, and generally acting like a bunch of babies. They were the exact opposite of Sissy Rae, who was wearing a frilly white party dress and a pink bow in her perfect curls.

Sissy Rae spotted Julia sitting near the toy box. "Down!" she whined. "Want to get down!"

"How about some food?" I suggested, hoping to distract her. "We've got your favorite—spinach with chocolate sauce."

Sissy Rae began to sob. "Dance!" she blubbered. "Want to dance with dat girl!"

Poor kid. She remembered the fun she'd had spinning and twirling with Julia last time, and she wanted to do it again. What was so terrible about that? "Sorry, kid," I said apologetically. "Your mom says no."

Sissy Rae threw back her head and cried harder. Julia noticed and toddled over. When Sissy Rae saw her, she leaned precariously over the edge of her high chair. "Dance!" she whined. "*Puh-leeze?*"

What was I supposed to do? If Violet walked in and saw Sissy Rae bawling, she'd have a fit. But she wouldn't be any happier if she found her little darling dancing with Julia. Then I had an idea. I'd let her down just long enough for Mom to whip up a few of her favorite food combinations, then I'd use the food to lure her back to her seat.

"Okay, Sissy Rae, here you go," I said, depositing her on the floor. "But you've got to promise to get back in the high chair when the food comes."

Sissy Rae didn't answer. She grabbed Julia's hand and began to wiggle. Soon the two of them were dipping and bouncing to the imaginary music inside their heads.

That was my cue to grab a passing busboy. "Quick, I need an order of grapes with ketchup, spinach with chocolate sauce, and . . ." Suddenly, I remembered Will's suggestion. ". . . french fries with maple syrup. Hurry!"

The busboy rolled his eyes. "Celebrities," he muttered. "They're all a little wacko." He wrote down the order and headed for the kitchen.

I looked up to see a woman, about sixty years old, with a lined face and an enormous black bouffant hairdo peering into the baby room. I cringed, thinking she must be one of Sissy Rae's relatives—a grandmother maybe, or an aunt— coming to bawl me out for letting Sissy Rae play with my sister. But of course that was silly. Violet hadn't brought anyone with her except Pearl Pendergast. As if to prove my point, the woman walked over to a bald baby who was sucking on a celery stick, cooed at him for a moment, then left.

A happy squeal from the corner made me turn around. Julia and Sissy Rae had danced their way over to the toy box and were now slithering around on the floor like a couple of hyperactive snakes. "No!" I cried, rushing toward them. "Sissy Rae, stand up. Your dress is going to get dirty."

"Go 'way," she said in a pouty voice.

"I can't go away," I answered, kneeling down to take her arm. "I'm supposed to be taking care of you."

"Go 'way!" she shouted, kicking her feet wildly. Both of her spotless patent-leather shoes flew off and hit me in the face.

"Hey," Jackson called from across the room, "I could use some help here!"

Now what? It wasn't fair to make Jackson feed and entertain nine kids all by himself, but if I left Sissy Rae alone, there was no telling what she might do.

"Puck, get over here!" Jackson shouted. "I've got three screaming toddlers and a baby with a raisin up his nose!"

"Don't move," I told Sissy Rae. "I'll be back in a flash with your food." Then I ran over to join Jackson.

We removed the raisin by sticking pepper in the kid's other nostril and making him sneeze, then sang a verse of "Gopher Guts" to cheer up the toddlers. When everything was back to normal, I jogged to the toy box, where I found Julia playing with Loola—alone. "What happened to Sissy Rae?" I demanded.

Julia pointed behind me. I spun around—then froze, too horrified to do anything but gape. The busboy had left Sissy Rae's food on her table while I was gone, and she had found it. Now she was sitting under the table with the plate in her lap, eating with her hands.

Please, I prayed, kneeling down to survey the damage, *tell me she didn't get ketchup on her dress.* But she'd done that, and much more. She had ketchup on her dress, maple syrup in her hair, and chocolate sauce all over her arms and legs. When she saw me, she looked up and smiled. "Fried taters 'n' syrup," she cooed. "Yum."

"Come on," I said, slipping my hands under her armpits and sliding her out from under the table, "we've got to get you cleaned up, and fast." I reached inside my apron pocket for a package of wet wipes, then stopped. Using them would be like trying to wipe up Niagara Falls with a Kleenex. I hoisted Sissy Rae into my arms and headed for the bathroom. "Jackson," I called across the room, "hold down the fort. I'll be right back."

The two single-person, unisex bathrooms were in a hallway off the front foyer. "Want taters 'n' syrup," Sissy Rae whined as I pulled open the closest door and dragged her inside.

"You can have a truckload of taters 'n' syrup as soon as I get you cleaned up," I said. I turned on the water, soaked a wad of paper towels, and began wiping her face.

"No!" she shrieked, kicking my shins with her tiny feet.

That's when I remembered her shoes were still back in the dining room somewhere. I let out a groan. Somehow I had to get Sissy Rae cleaned up, comb her hair, and put her shoes back on before Violet came looking for her.

Suddenly, I heard a glass-shattering shriek coming from out in the foyer. I knew instantly it was Violet Comstock. "Where is my baby?" she bellowed.

My stomach started to churn. I wiped faster, and Sissy Rae responded by throwing herself onto the bathroom floor. A second later, I heard my father's voice. "Don't worry, Mrs. Comstock, we'll find her. I'm sure there's a perfectly reasonable explanation for this."

Yeah, I thought, *like your son screwed up, big time.* My stomach churned faster, like a food processor in overdrive. Then the churning moved lower, and a horrible realization came to me. The two Triple-Mondo-Mega Cheeseburgers I'd eaten this afternoon were ready to come out. I had to go to the bathroom. *Now!*

What was I going to do? I couldn't go while Sissy Rae was there. It would be way too embarrassing, and Sissy Rae could very well take advantage of the situation and escape.

When Violet found her, unsupervised and covered with food, I'd be as good as dead.

The only other possibility was to find someone to watch Sissy Rae while I used the other bathroom. But who? I couldn't ask Dad because he was with Violet Comstock. I couldn't ask Jackson because he was already too busy in the baby room, the first place Dad and Violet would go to look for Sissy Rae.

That left Mom and Will. But in order to ask them, I'd have to schlep Sissy Rae through the lobby and the adult room into the kitchen, explain the situation, then run back to the bathroom again. Judging by the way my insides were feeling, I couldn't wait that long.

Finally, I did the only thing I could think of. I grabbed the sash on the back of Sissy Rae's dress and tied it to the drainpipe underneath the sink. "Don't cry, Sissy Rae," I said in what I hoped was a soothing voice. "I'll be back before you can say spinach with chocolate sauce." Then I left her in the bathroom, ducked next door, and took care of business.

Minutes later, I flushed the toilet and hurried back to finish cleaning off Sissy Rae. But when I opened the bathroom door, my heart skipped a beat and my legs went weak. The bathroom was empty. Sissy Rae was gone!

Chapter
7

My mind was reeling. Had Sissy Rae managed to untie her sash and run outside? Or had someone—a customer, or even Violet herself—opened the bathroom door and found her?

For a fleeting moment, I thought maybe Sissy Rae had climbed out the window above the toilet. But then I realized that was impossible. The window was almost five feet above the toilet seat. There was no way Sissy Rae could get up there without a ladder. The kid was barely three feet tall!

I took a deep breath and tried to think. If I could just track down Sissy Rae, take her back to Violet, and explain that I had merely been cleaning food off her little darling's precious legs, nobody could get *too* mad at me, could they? Yeah, right. Who was I kidding? Violet would be furious. Still, it would be better than letting her find Sissy Rae wandering through the restaurant all alone.

I pushed open the bathroom door. At the same moment, someone pulled from the outside. I fell forward—and found myself face-to-face with Jackson.

"I've been looking all over for you," he said anxiously. "Have you seen Sissy Rae? She's not in the baby room."

"I know," I said. I gave him a brief rundown of the situation.

"We've got to find her!" he cried.

"What do you think I'm trying to do? Come on!"

We checked all the closets in the hallway, then looked in the foyer. Jackson walked out the front door to search the street. "Sissy Rae!" I heard him calling. "Are you out here? We have frozen yogurt and soy sauce for you."

Finally, he walked back inside and shook his head. "No luck. Let's try the baby room."

We peeked inside, but Dad was in there, ripping the place apart with Violet and Pearl Pendergast while the babies watched with interest. "They haven't found her yet," I said as we ducked back into the foyer. "That means there's still hope."

"Come on, let's try the adult room," Jackson said.

We walked through the crowded room, trying not to arouse suspicion among the diners as we casually peeked under the tables and behind the potted plants.

"There's nowhere left except the kitchen," Jackson said at last. "And I'm sure your mom or Will would know if she was in there."

"We might as well take a look," I replied, hoping against hope that Jackson was wrong.

We walked in to find a huge cloud of black smoke hanging in the air. Mom was standing at the stove, cooking pasta with a wet towel over her mouth and nose. "What happened?" I asked, stifling a cough.

"The oven overheated and a soufflé caught fire," Mom said. "Fortunately, Will thought fast. He disconnected the smoke alarm before it could go off and scare the customers, then he put out the fire with the fire extinguisher. The only problem is, he inhaled a lot of smoke in the process.

He was coughing like crazy, so I sent him home."

I glanced at the open oven. It was splattered with bits of burned soufflé and foam. "So . . . I guess Sissy Rae hasn't been in here, huh?"

"Sissy Rae?" Mom frowned as she turned to look at Jackson and me. "Wait a minute. What are you boys doing in here? Why aren't you in the baby room with—"

"Have you seen Sissy Rae?" Dad cried, bursting through the kitchen door. He looked at my mother imploringly. "Please tell me she's in here."

"What in the world is going on?" Mom asked impatiently.

Before anyone could answer, Violet and Pearl Pendergast barged into the kitchen, practically knocking Dad over. "Did you find her?" Violet demanded.

"Not yet," he admitted, "but I'm sure—"

"This is an outrage!" Pearl growled. "A disgrace!"

"Will someone please tell me what's going on?" Mom almost shouted.

"It—it's my fault," I said, choking out the words. "Sissy Rae got food all over her and I took her to the bathroom to clean her off. But then I had to . . . well, you know, go. So I ran to the other bathroom, but when I came back—"

"You left her alone?" Violet cried. "You idiot! That baby is a major talent, a star. What were you thinking?"

"Please, Mrs. Comstock, there's no need to be insulting," Dad said. "Puck may have made a mistake in judgment, but he was only trying to keep you—"

"She could be anywhere!" Violet wailed, ignoring my father. "She could be lost, or kidnapped—or dead!"

"I'm calling the police," Pearl Pendergast announced, pulling a cellular phone out of her purse. She dialed 911. "Hello, this is an emergency. I'd like to report a disappearance."

Dad ran his hands over his face and let out a groan. "Jackson, get back to the baby room and take care of the kids," he said. "Sandy, go on with your cooking." He turned to me. "Come with me, Puck. We've got to find that kid before the cops show up."

Dad and I rushed through the restaurant, frantically searching for Sissy Rae. Naturally, the other diners were beginning to notice that something was wrong. Each time my father and I walked through the adult room, someone stopped him to complain about the slow service or to ask what all the commotion was about.

"We're a little short-handed tonight, that's all," Dad said in his most soothing voice. "Please accept our apology and a free dessert, courtesy of the management."

That kept everyone happy for a while, but when the cops arrived—three uniformed officers and one plain-clothed detective—there was no hiding the fact that something was seriously wrong. Dad, Violet, Pearl Pendergast, and I all ran to the front door to meet them.

"I'm Captain Nishio," the detective said. He was a muscular Asian guy with a buzz cut and a look in his eyes that seemed to say, *You can't put one over on me.* "Would someone like to tell me what happened?" he asked.

Everyone started talking at once. Dad was trying to act like nothing was wrong, I was explaining about leaving Sissy Rae in the bathroom, Violet was wailing hysterically about her famous baby, and Pearl was demanding immediate justice.

"Check the bathrooms," Captain Nishio told one of his men when we'd finally stopped talking. The officer ran off down the hall. Nishio turned to Violet. "Do you have a picture of your daughter?"

She hesitated, but Pearl pulled an autographed publicity

photo from her purse. Nishio handed it to the two remaining officers and said, "Search the restaurant."

"Act casual," Dad called as the officers walked away. "I don't want to upset the other customers." Poor Dad. He was so freaked out he didn't seem to realize that no matter how casual the police officers acted, the customers were going to notice them and wonder what the heck was going on.

"I apologize for the inconvenience, Mr. Rosen," Captain Nishio said, "but if we don't find the little girl immediately, I'm going to have to question everyone who was in this restaurant at the time of her disappearance."

"But you've *got* to find her," Violet sobbed. "She has commitments!"

"She's taping her first TV show next month," Pearl explained. "Captain, that child is worth millions." She pulled a cigarette from her purse and lit up. "I was going to quit," she fussed, "but I'm just too upset." She inhaled so hard that half the cigarette turned to ash.

"Captain, look," one of the officers called, hurrying down the hallway. With rubber-gloved hands, he held up a crumpled piece of paper. I leaned closer to look. The paper was covered with letters, some handwritten, some cut out of magazines and newspapers.

SISSY RAE IS SAFE AND HAPPY, the note read. DON'T BOTHER LOOKING FOR HER.

"I knew it!" Violet shrieked. "My baby's been kidnapped!"

"Then why doesn't the note say anything about money?" my father asked.

"How should I know?" Violet cried. "All I know is this moron here left her alone and some maniac took her." She pointed at me with such an accusing look, I wasn't sure if she thought I was the moron or the maniac. Maybe both.

"We may receive more notes in the future," Captain Nishio said. "Or this may not have anything to do with money. Sissy Rae's kidnapper could be a crazed fan." He turned to the officer. "Where did you find this paper?"

"It was shoved between the window and the sill in the first bathroom," he answered.

"Was the window open?"

The officer shook his head. "Closed and latched from the inside."

"Then the girl wasn't taken through the window— unless someone in the bathroom lifted her out and then closed it again." He turned to me. "According to your story, you were in the other bathroom when Sissy Rae was taken. Now think carefully. Did you hear anything? Shouts, crying, any sounds of a struggle?"

I thought it over. "No, sir. I didn't hear a thing."

Captain Nishio frowned. "That means the kidnapper must have covered Sissy Rae's mouth and carried her out of the bathroom before she could cry out. Either that, or she was taken by someone she wasn't afraid of. Someone she already knew . . ." He stared at me long and hard.

"What are you getting at?" my father asked uneasily.

Before Captain Nishio could answer, two parents walked out from the adult room. "What's going on?" the mother asked. "What are the police doing here?"

"We can't divulge any information at this time," Captain Nishio said. "Please go on with your dinner."

The parents glanced at each other. "I don't like the looks of this," the father said. "Get little Jimmy and let's go home."

"Wait!" Dad cried, running after them as they walked toward the baby room. "Don't go. Please allow me to get you a complimentary dessert. How about a cappuccino? Maybe an espresso?"

But the man and woman kept walking. Now more parents were filing out of the adult room and demanding to know what was going on. Jackson heard the commotion and came out of the baby room carrying a fussy toddler in each arm. At the same time, the two officers who had been searching the building returned, along with my mother and Julia. Mom rushed to my dad's side and took his arm, while Julia stared at the police officers with fascination.

"We can't find any sign of her," one of the officers reported.

Nishio nodded. "Guard the doors. No one leaves this building until we've questioned them."

The three officers headed for the front door, but before they could get there, a horde of reporters with TV cameras and microphones burst into the restaurant. They were all shouting at once.

"Is it true Sissy Rae Comstock has disappeared?"

"When was she last seen?"

"Violet, can you tell us what you're feeling right now?"

"Mr. Rosen, what exactly happened here tonight?"

Captain Nishio scowled. "Get them out of here," he ordered his men.

"Wait!" Pearl cried. "I'm Pearl Pendergast, Sissy Rae's agent." The reporters pressed forward eagerly as Pearl lit a cigarette and said, "Tonight in this restaurant, America's sweetheart, Sissy Rae Comstock, was kidnapped. I'm sure I speak for everyone when I say, 'Be brave, Sissy Rae. We're going to find you if it's the last thing we do.'" She turned to Violet and asked gently, "Do you feel strong enough to speak to the American public, hon?"

Strong enough? Violet looked like a tiger as she growled, "I hold this restaurant and its owners personally responsible for what's happened to my little girl. As soon as

Sissy Rae is returned to me, I plan to sue them for all they're worth!"

"Okay, that's enough!" Captain Nishio barked. "You've got your story, folks. Now I want the media out of here immediately!"

While the officers rounded up the reporters and forced them out the door, I glanced over at my parents. They looked stunned, and I knew what they were thinking. If Violet took them to court and won—a good possibility, since she had left Sissy Rae in their care—Mom and Dad would lose the restaurant, not to mention every penny they owned.

I felt a lump forming in my throat. I wanted to tell my parents I was sorry. I wanted to explain what had happened and let them know I felt like a total loser for screwing up and letting them down. But before I could open my mouth, Captain Nishio began shouting orders, telling everyone to line up for questioning and promising all the parents they'd be home with their babies within the hour.

Then he turned to me. "What's your name, son?"

"P-Puck," I stammered. "Puck Rosen."

"Puck, I want you to show me those bathrooms. Then you're going to tell me everything that happened, from the moment you set foot in this restaurant tonight right up until the instant you saw me walk through the front door. You got that?"

I looked up at him. His eyes seemed to be staring right through my skull into my brain. "I got it, sir," I gulped.

The customers were questioned and sent home within the hour, just as Captain Nishio had promised. But by the time the police had questioned Mom, Dad, Violet, Pearl, Jackson, the waiters and busboys, and me, it was almost midnight. I don't know what he asked the others—he took each of us into a small room at the back of the restaurant for privacy—but he asked me *everything*. The guy was so thorough, he even wanted to know how many paper towels I'd used to clean Sissy Rae and whether or not I'd flushed the toilet after I went to the bathroom. As if I could remember! I was so exhausted and upset, I could barely remember Sissy Rae's last name.

Finally, it was over. The busboys left, and Nishio asked one of the officers to escort Violet and Pearl to their cars. Then he turned to Mom and Dad. "I'm sorry I had to put you through all this," he said. "I know it must have been a difficult evening for you."

"It doesn't matter," Dad answered. "All that matters is that you find Sissy Rae."

"We will," he said confidently. "But until we do, don't leave town. Also, you might want to hire a good lawyer."

Mom nodded. "If Violet Comstock takes us to court, we're going to need an entire team of lawyers to defend ourselves."

"That wasn't what I meant," Nishio said. "I'm advising you to hire a good criminal lawyer for you and your son."

"What?" Dad gasped. "But why?"

"As of tonight," the captain replied, "the three of you are our most likely suspects."

Chapter
8

"Okay, I admit I wasn't thrilled when Mom and Dad opened Baby Bistro," I said glumly, "but I never meant to put them out of business."

It was the day after Sissy Rae's kidnapping, and I was sitting in Jackson's bedroom, absentmindedly leafing through a mountain biking magazine. My parents had sent me to Jackson's house to get me away from the reporters and photographers who were hanging around our house. Every time Mom, Dad, or I went outside or even walked near a window, they would snap photos and shout questions at us, stuff like, "Why did you leave Sissy Rae alone, Puck?" and "Is it true the cops think you did it?"

"Baby Bistro hasn't gone belly-up yet," Jackson said, patting me on the back, "and even if it does, it won't be your fault. I mean, you had to go to the bathroom and there was no one around to watch Sissy Rae, right? I would have done the same thing if it had been me."

"But it wasn't you. It was *me,* and now Sissy Rae has disappeared, my parents are about to be sued, and Captain Nishio thinks we're hiding Sissy Rae in our basement."

"Doesn't he realize your house doesn't have a basement?" Jackson joked.

"This is serious," I told him. "A team of officers showed up at our house this morning with a warrant and searched the place from top to bottom."

"Unreal," Jackson said, shaking his head. "How could anyone suspect you and your parents of kidnapping Sissy Rae? I mean, you've already got one toddler in your house. You'd be crazy to want another."

"Tell that to Captain Nishio," I replied. "According to him, everyone who was in the restaurant last night has an alibi except me. You and the busboys were in the baby room at the time of the kidnapping. All the parents and waiters were in the adult room. Dad was there too, and Mom and Will were in the kitchen. That leaves me. Only Nishio doesn't think a kid could plan and carry out a kidnapping alone, so he figures my parents must be involved, too."

"Wait a minute," Jackson said, leaning forward. "Your mother told us she sent Will home because he had inhaled a lot of smoke, right? Maybe he left through the back door, came in again through the front door, and snatched Sissy Rae."

I shook my head. "Nice try, but according to Mom, Will left the restaurant about two minutes before we walked into the kitchen. Sissy Rae had already disappeared by that time."

"But I still don't see why the cops suspect *you*," Jackson said. "You weren't even in the same room with Sissy Rae when she vanished."

I shrugged. "I don't think Nishio believes my story. Let's face it, it *is* kind of bizarre that I had to go to the bathroom in the middle of cleaning up Sissy Rae, and that I left her tied to the sink, and that someone chose that exact moment to grab her. If I didn't know it was true, I wouldn't believe it myself."

Jackson let out a sigh. "This is getting depressing. Let's hit the trail and forget the whole thing."

I shook my head. "I'm too bummed out to go mountain biking. Anyway, I think the tabloid reporters followed me here. If we go outside, they'll be all over us."

"Then let's check out Mom and Dad's workshop," Jackson suggested.

In spite of my troubles, I perked up. Zeke and Winnie's workshop was one of the coolest places on earth, and whenever Jackson and I were given permission to spend time there, we jumped at the chance. Usually that happened when his folks were between projects, or when they were taking a lunch break. Then they let us come in and try on the masks, fool around with the makeup and wigs, and manipulate the mechanical body parts.

But today Jackson's parents were out at the movies. "Are you sure we're allowed to go in there?" I asked.

"You need to get your mind off this whole Sissy Rae thing," Jackson said reassuringly. "If my parents were here, I know they'd say yes."

"Well, okay." I allowed myself a small smile. "Lead the way."

I followed Jackson down the hall to the room that served as the main workshop for Duprey Productions. He opened the door and turned on the light. As always, a delightful shiver went down my spine as I gazed at the bloody dummies, deformed plastic heads, and metallic robot arms that lay strewn about the room.

"Check this out," Jackson said, picking up one of the alien insect masks his parents were creating for the sci-fi flick *Creepy Crawly*. He pulled it over his head and advanced toward me menacingly. "Yum, Earth brains! My favorite!" he exclaimed. "Come here, kid. Slurp! Slurp!"

I laughed and shoved him away. "The scary thing is, compared to your normal face, that mask looks pretty good."

He snickered and pulled it off. Then he walked over to a tall bookshelf that was filled with cases of movie makeup and jars of fake blood. "Let's turn ourselves into a couple of ghouls, then go outside and scare the pants off those reporter guys."

"I can see the headlines now," I chuckled. "HALF-BOY, HALF-VAMPIRE ADMITS, 'I SUCKED SISSY RAE'S BLOOD.'"

Jackson cracked up, then reached for a makeup case. He sat down at one of the workbenches and took a mirror out of the case. I grabbed a jar of fake blood off the shelf and joined him. Soon we were busy turning ourselves into deformed, blood-splattered ghouls. In fact, we were so absorbed in our work, we didn't notice that Jackson's cat, Benny, had slinked into the room and was sniffing through the clutter for scraps of leftover food.

"MEE-OOW!"

I looked up just in time to see Benny, a plate, and a half-eaten ham sandwich fall off the bookcase. Benny hit the floor on all four paws and streaked out of the room like a missile. The ham sandwich landed on Jackson's head, and the plate crashed against a dummy, which tipped forward into my lap.

I let out a gasp and jumped to my feet. The dummy fell to the floor with a bang. I stood there staring at it, my heart pounding against my ribs like a pile driver. Then I turned and saw Jackson with a slice of moldy ham plastered against his cheek, and cracked up.

"That stupid cat!" he gulped, peeling the ham off his face. "He scared me half to death!"

"Me, too." I waited until my heartbeat was back to something resembling normal. Then I knelt down and picked up the dummy. It was a teenage boy in a trench coat and fedora. "Who's this guy supposed to be?"

"It's a stunt dummy my folks are creating for an upcoming movie called *The Undercover Kids*," Jackson replied. "Something about a couple of teenage geniuses who use their superior brainpower to solve crimes."

Suddenly I had an idea. "Hey," I said, "maybe *we* could do that."

"Solve crimes?"

"Just one. I want to find out who kidnapped Sissy Rae Comstock."

"Nice idea," Jackson said, "but don't forget, we're not geniuses."

"Maybe not, but why should we wait around for the cops to figure out who took Sissy Rae? Let's find out for ourselves—or try anyway. Who knows? We might uncover a clue that leads to the real kidnapper—and proves that my parents and I are innocent."

Jackson didn't have to think it over. "When do we start?" he asked eagerly.

"Right now," I said. "Your parents own more videos than the local video store. Let's watch some famous crime movies and start learning how to think like detectives. Then we can decide what—or who—to investigate first."

Jackson grinned. "You pick the videos, I'll get the junk food. It's couch-potato time."

"Let's face it, Violet Comstock is not your typical mother," I said as I skipped my bike off the curb and swerved around a parked car. "I think she views Sissy Rae more like a meal ticket than a daughter."

Jackson nodded as he pedaled up beside me. "Did you notice how she hesitated when Captain Nishio asked if she had a photo of Sissy Rae? What mom doesn't carry a picture of her own kid in her wallet?"

It was the next day, and Jackson and I were on our way to the Comstock house to do a little investigating. Based on the stuff we'd learned during yesterday's detective-movie marathon, we figured Violet Comstock had the best motive for kidnapping—or pretending to kidnap—Sissy Rae. In a word, publicity.

Ever since she'd disappeared, Sissy Rae's photo had been plastered across every newspaper and magazine in the country, and her face had appeared on the TV news morning, noon, and night. In a matter of hours, the entire country had become obsessed with finding Sissy Rae. When she finally turned up, she was going to be a national hero—not a bad thing to be if you were just about to launch a new TV show.

"The more I think about it, the more I'm convinced Violet staged the kidnapping," I said as we pedaled past a sign that read WELCOME TO BEVERLY HILLS. "The only question is, where is she hiding her?"

"That's what we've got to find out," Jackson said. He stopped and unfolded his L.A. map. "Two more blocks, then turn right."

Figuring out where Violet and Sissy Rae lived had been easy. We'd simply walked outside my house and told the first reporter we saw that we would tell him a couple of juicy Sissy Rae stories in return for her address. Five minutes later, the reporter knew that Sissy Rae liked spinach with chocolate sauce and dancing to "Pop Goes the Weasel," and we knew that Violet lived at 1314 Palm Drive.

When we reached the house—an enormous Colonial-style mansion with a silver Jaguar parked in the driveway—I skidded to a halt and let out a groan. There was a pack of reporters hanging out at the curb, just like at our house. "How can we get any investigating done with them here?" I asked Jackson. "Once they spot us, they'll never leave us alone."

"I think you're forgetting something," he replied. "Have you looked in a mirror lately?"

How could I have forgotten? In order to make sure we weren't recognized while we snooped around, we had borrowed some of Zeke and Winnie's movie makeup and disguised ourselves. I was wearing a curly brown wig over my straight blond hair, my nose was twice as broad as normal, and I had a fake scar on my chin.

"You really think they won't recognize me?" I asked, nervously fingering my latex nose.

Jackson laughed. "Are you kidding? You look like an escapee from reform school. How about me?"

I glanced at the shaggy red wig that hid his short black hair, the blue contacts that covered his brown eyes, and the pale makeup that we'd used to turn his skin about three shades lighter. "I'd never recognize you in a million years."

"Good. Now let's get to work."

We didn't have much of a game plan. We just figured we'd snoop around and see if we could uncover some clues. But first we had to make sure Violet wasn't in the house. We hid our bikes in the bushes across the street, then walked up to the front door and rang the bell. The reporters glanced at us, but didn't even bother to snap a photo. Unbelievable! They really didn't recognize us.

"We're home free," Jackson whispered when no one answered the door. "Let's go around back and start investigating."

We walked off down the street as if we were leaving, but when we got to the corner, we sneaked around to the back of the house. The yard was surrounded by a high wooden fence, but to our surprise, there was a gate at the back and it was unlocked. "This is almost too easy," I said as we headed into the yard.

The first thing we noticed was the pool. It was big and kidney-shaped and surrounded by expensive lawn furniture. The rest of the yard was covered with perfectly manicured grass. Other than a small white shed and a couple of palm trees, the yard was empty.

"There's something kind of eerie about this place," I said. "I mean, it's so quiet. More like a cemetery than a backyard."

"And where are the toys?" Jackson asked. "At your house, I can barely walk two feet without tripping over a doll or a block or a puzzle piece. I don't see any kid stuff—outside *or* inside."

I followed his pointing finger to the French doors that lined the back of the house. We walked closer and peered through the panes. The rooms were filled with gaudy furniture and big glass sculptures. There wasn't a speck of dust—or a toy—in sight.

"And I thought *your* parents were neat freaks!" Jackson exclaimed. "At least they let Julia carry her toys around the house. Violet must make Sissy Rae keep them all in her—"

Jackson's voice cut off as a black-haired woman in a hairnet and a pink uniform walked into the dining room. When she caught sight of us, she leaped backward and clutched her heart. "*Dios mío!*" she cried.

I froze, then took a step backward, ready to hightail it out of there. But it was too late. Within seconds the woman had rushed to the French doors and flung them open. Now she was sizing us up with her dark, suspicious eyes.

"What do you want?" she demanded in a Spanish accent. "You look too young to be reporters or photographers, but who knows? Maybe the newspapers hired you to dig up more dirt on Sissy Rae, *verdad*?"

"Uh . . . er . . . no, ma'am," I stammered. I glanced at the logo on her uniform: MESS-BUSTERS HOUSECLEANING SERVICE. "We . . . we're not from the newspapers. We're . . . uh . . . uh . . ."

"The pool boys," Jackson blurted out. "It's our summer job. We're here to clean Mrs. Comstock's pool."

"That's right," I agreed, nodding vigorously. "Ask Mrs. Comstock if you don't believe us. She hired us last week."

"Señora Comstock is not home," the cleaning woman replied. She looked us up and down, her eyes narrowing. "Well, you go ahead," she said at last. "But remember, boys, Consuela is watching." She reached into her pocket and pulled out a small, deadly looking handgun.

My heart leaped into my throat, then flopped around inside my chest like a hyperactive guppy. I opened my mouth to speak, but Consuela held up her hand for silence. "Any funny business," she said with a thin smile, "and I shoot first, ask questions later."

Chapter 9

Consuela turned away, but she left the French doors open. "Do you know anything about cleaning pools?" I whispered as Jackson and I walked through the yard.

"Not a thing," he admitted.

"Great. Just great. What do we do now?"

"Let's check the shed. There's bound to be some pool-cleaning equipment in there. All we have to do is look busy until she stops watching us, then make a run for it."

I glanced over my shoulder. Consuela was sitting at the dining room table, watching us like a hungry hawk checking out a couple of mice. "Let's just pray she's not very good at hitting a moving target," I said.

We opened the shed and found a long-handled brush and net. We'd seen the lifeguards at the YMCA use them, so we knew what to do. Jackson plunged the brush into the water and began to scrub the floor and the walls of the pool. I took the net and scooped leaves off the surface.

"Is she still watching us?" I asked after I'd bagged what seemed like my hundredth leaf.

"Like a pitcher eyeing a runner on first base."

I frowned. "What else do pool guys do?"

"Put chlorine in the water, I guess," he answered. "Let's check the shed and see what we can find."

We walked back to the shed and looked around. There was all kinds of junk in there—shovels, rakes, flowerpots, potting soil, and some unmarked cardboard boxes. I thought about opening them—after all, we were supposed to be looking for clues—but I didn't have the nerve. My mind was stuck on the gun in Consuela's pocket and what she might do with it if she found us snooping around in Violet's private stuff.

I glanced over at Jackson. He was rooting around in the corner, reading the labels on some dusty old plastic containers. "I found some," he said, holding up a tub of powdered chlorine. "It's got a scoop in it and everything."

We hurried back to the pool. Consuela was still watching us from her chair in the dining room. We waved and grinned.

"Chlorine," I explained, pointing to it. I turned to Jackson. "How much should we put in?"

"I don't know. A few scoopfuls, I guess." He grabbed the scoop and dumped in a cup's worth. "Is the water supposed to look clearer?" he asked.

I shrugged. "Who knows? It looks just the same to me."

"Let's add some more," he suggested. He sprinkled another two scoopfuls into the water, then paused and added one more for good measure.

"Okay, that's enough," I said. "Now let's get out of here before that cleaning lady uses our butts for target practice."

"We're going now, Consuela," Jackson called as I put the plastic tub back in the shed, "so, uh, don't shoot us, okay?"

Consuela walked out the French doors. To my amazement, she was smiling. "Boys, you don't have to be afraid of me. You see this gun?" My knees went limp as she pulled it out of her pocket again. "It shoots blanks only. Señora Comstock gave it to me after Sissy Rae was kidnapped. She said, 'Don't let strangers in the yard.' But I see now you are good pool boys, just like you told me."

"Blanks?" I repeated weakly.

She nodded. "Come in. I'll get you some lemonade. It's hot today, no?"

Jackson and I looked at each other. Was she telling the truth, or was this a trick to make us lower our guard before she blasted us full of lead? She headed back inside. We hesitated, then followed her warily.

A few moments later, Consuela was handing us tall glasses of lemonade and crushed ice. "Come, we sit," she said, lowering herself into a dining room chair. We sat across from her. "Ah, this is heaven," she said, taking a sip. "I've been on my feet since seven o'clock this morning. That Señora Comstock, she is a slave driver."

I stared at Consuela, stunned. A few minutes ago, she had seemed like a dangerous psychopath. Now she was acting like a regular person. I decided to take a chance and ask her a couple of questions. "How long have you worked for Mrs. Comstock?"

"Six months. Ever since she came to L.A."

"So you know Sissy Rae," Jackson said, taking my lead.

"Oh, you bet. Sweet little girl, but that mama of hers doesn't understand what it means to be a baby. All day long she makes Sissy Rae work. First the singing lessons, then the dance lessons, then the acting. In the afternoon, the hairdresser comes to do the little girl's hair, and the seamstress comes to make her clothes. Señora Comstock even makes the baby wear makeup."

"Where's Sissy Rae's father?" I asked.

"It's a sad, sad story. Señora Comstock said her husband

ran out on them a year ago. The police found him dead three months later in a homeless shelter in Chicago." She shook her head. "Poor Sissy Rae. She must miss her papa *mucho*."

Well, that explained why Sissy Rae was always asking for her father. Poor kid. Between losing her dad and being forced to perform like a trained seal in TV commercials, it was no wonder she was depressed.

On the other hand, hearing about Mr. Comstock made me feel a little more sympathetic toward Violet. I mean, it couldn't have been easy being married to a loser like that, and everyone knows that raising a kid alone is no picnic either. Violet probably jumped at the chance to have her daughter make it in show biz.

"I must go now," Consuela said, standing up. "I've got a house to clean on Beverly Drive." She took our lemonade glasses into the kitchen, then bustled through the French doors. "Come, boys. Señora Comstock said I should be extra careful to lock up tight when I leave."

We followed her through the doors and out the gate. She walked off toward Palm Drive and was soon spotted by the reporters. In an instant they had surrounded her and were shouting questions about Violet and Sissy Rae.

"Well, I guess we've found out everything we can around here," I said.

"Don't bet on it," Jackson replied. "I unlocked the French doors on my way out."

"Wow, maybe you *are* a genius," I said, slapping him a high five.

We glanced up and down the street to make sure the reporters weren't watching us, then hurried back into the yard. Sure enough, the back door was open. We grinned at each other and walked inside.

The house was as cold and quiet as a funeral parlor. We walked through the living room, down the hall, and into Sissy Rae's bedroom. The walls were pink, and so were the frilly curtains and bedspread. The only toy in sight was a formal dollhouse and one dressed-up, spotlessly clean doll. Even more amazing, the wall-to-wall carpeting was pure white.

"Can you imagine if Julia had white carpeting on her floor?" I exclaimed. "In two days it would be covered with grape jelly, dirt, crayons, and who knows what else!"

"The more I learn about Violet," Jackson said, "the more I'm convinced she arranged for Sissy Rae to be kidnapped as a publicity stunt. That woman will stop at nothing to turn her kid into a superstar."

"Maybe," I replied, "but after talking to Consuela, it seems to me our list of possible suspects just got longer. There's Sissy Rae's dance teacher, her singing teacher, her acting teacher, not to mention her hairdresser and seamstress. They all knew Sissy Rae's schedule, and they all knew she was making big bucks."

"But there hasn't been a ransom note," Jackson argued as we moved on to Violet's bedroom. "That means money isn't the motive, not directly anyway."

"You may be right," I said, leafing through the bills and letters on Violet's dresser, "but I still wouldn't rule out anyone who works for Violet—not even Consuela. Who knows? The kidnapper might be waiting until everyone is at wit's end before he sends the ransom note."

Jackson didn't answer. He was staring at a piece of paper on Violet's bedside table. "Hey, check this out," he said, holding it up. "Have you ever seen this handwriting before?"

I glanced at the large, curving letters. They looked oddly

familiar. "The kidnapper's note!" I cried at last. "The handwritten parts looked exactly like this!" I grabbed the paper out of Jackson's hand and read it. It was a memo about one of Sissy Rae's upcoming Puff 'N' Soft commercials. "Pearl Pendergast!" I gasped, reading the signature at the bottom.

"I wonder if Captain Nishio knows about this," Jackson said.

"I think we'd better tell him. But first, let's go over to Pearl Pendergast's office and do a little investigating. If we can uncover some more evidence that leads to her, we'll have this case wrapped up."

Jackson grinned. "You know, I think we're really getting the hang of this detective stuff." We returned the memo to Violet's bedside table and strolled back to the dining room. "How about another glass of lemonade, Sherlock?"

"Do you think we should?"

He shrugged. "Why not? After cleaning Violet's pool, we deserve it."

"You've got a point there. Lead the way, Watson."

We walked into the kitchen, and Jackson took the pitcher out of the refrigerator. I was just about to pour the lemonade into our old glasses when I heard the front door open. I gasped, then turned to Jackson.

"Do you hear what I hear?" I whispered. There were footsteps moving through the house, and they were coming our way!

"Let's get out of here!" he hissed.

We ran out the back door just as Violet walked into the dining room. She let out a shriek, and I picked up speed. A second later my foot hit a patch of wet concrete at the edge of the pool and I started to slide. I tried to right myself, whacked into a lawn chair, and toppled into the water.

Instantly my eyes began to burn, and I knew we'd put in too much chlorine. I shot to the surface, then gasped as I saw a hairy brown lump pop out of the water beside me. Was it a coconut? A dead raccoon? I looked closer. It was my wig!

I grabbed the wig just as Violet flung open the back door. Quickly, I plunged back beneath the water, jammed the wig onto my head, and swam to the edge of the pool. As I scrambled up the stairs, I heard her shouting.

"Stop! Do you hear me? Stop or I'll shoot!"

It was the second time in one day I'd been threatened with a gun, only this time I was pretty sure the bullets were real. I took off like the Road Runner with Wile E. Coyote on his tail.

Jackson was hiding behind the gate, holding it open for me. I shot through it, and together we sprinted back to Palm Drive to retrieve our bikes.

We hadn't gone ten steps before the reporters appeared at the corner. They must have heard Violet's screams and come to see what was going on. When they saw us running toward them, looking like a couple of convicts with a pack of bloodhounds on our tails, they started snapping photographs.

"Keep your head low," Jackson warned. "If they recognize us, we're sunk."

We didn't have to worry. A second later Violet ran out of the gate, waving her gun and screeching, "I'm calling the cops!" Instantly the reporters forgot about us and turned their cameras on her.

We raced to the bushes across the street and grabbed our bikes. The last thing we saw was Violet shooting her gun into the air and the reporters screaming as they threw themselves to the ground. Then we took off down Palm Drive, dodging cars and hopping curbs as we headed for home.

Chapter
10

"I'm burning up!" I cried as we ran into my house. Pepperoni scampered after us, barking and growling like we were a couple of strangers. "My skin feels fried and my eyes are stinging like crazy."

"It must be the chlorine," Jackson said, pushing Pepperoni away. "Jump in the shower and see if you can wash it off."

I jogged into the bathroom and glanced in the mirror—then did a doubletake. I had completely forgotten that I was still wearing my disguise. No wonder Pepperoni was barking at us! My wig was on crooked and my latex nose was peeling off. I pulled off the wig—and screamed.

"My hair is green!"

Jackson hurried into the bathroom. He took one look at me and burst out laughing. "It's the chlorine. Oh, Puck, you look ridiculous!"

"Your sympathy is truly touching," I said as I threw off my chlorine-bleached clothes and stepped into the shower. I cupped my hands together to catch the water and let it wash over my eyes. Then I shampooed my hair and scrubbed my skin with lots of soap.

While I worked, I thought about Violet. Had she recognized us? It didn't seem likely. Still, I couldn't help worrying. It was bad enough that I was under suspicion for kidnapping. I didn't want the cops to add breaking and entering to my list of crimes.

After about fifteen minutes in the shower, I began to feel almost normal. I got out and toweled off. But when I looked in the mirror, my heart sank. My hair was still green!

"What do I do now?" I asked, walking out of the bathroom with a towel around me. I found Jackson (minus his disguise) in the living room with my mother, my father, and Julia. When they saw me, their mouths fell open.

"What happened to you?" Mom cried.

"Hair green, Uck," Julia announced brightly.

"I fell in a pool," I said, ignoring her.

"What pool?" Dad asked.

Somehow I didn't think Dad really wanted to hear the truth. "Uh . . . we were riding our bikes and uh . . . we met this kid whose lives on the other side of the canyon. We were all hot and tired so he invited us to his house for a swim."

"Only they'd accidentally put too much chlorine in the water," Jackson added, "and I guess it turned Puck's hair green."

"But why isn't your hair green?" Dad asked, eyeing him curiously.

Mom had the answer to that. "Jackson's hair is too dark. Chlorine burn only discolors blond hair. It happened to me once when I was a teenager."

Julia giggled. "Green hair," she said. "Funny."

"Yeah, right." I turned to Mom. "How do I get rid of it?"

"There's a special shampoo to wash out chlorine," she

replied. "We'll buy a bottle on the way to the restaurant. You can wash your hair in the restroom sink."

Only it turned out that none of the drug stores on the way to Baby Bistro had any anti-chlorine shampoo, so I had to spend the entire evening with green hair. Naturally, all the parents commented on my weird look. Some of them even complained they didn't want their children being cared for by a punk rocker. Apparently the babies agreed, because half of them took one look at me and burst out crying. And then there was Julia, who followed me around all evening, pointing at my head and saying, "Uck have green hair!"

"Can't you shut her up?" I begged when my dad stopped by the baby room to see how things were going.

"Hang in there," he said, ruffling my grasslike locks. "We'll buy you some of that shampoo on the way home."

"Too bad," Jackson remarked as he breezed past me with a plate of watermelon slices. "The alien look suits you, Puck."

The next morning I was in the shower, giving my hair a good scrubbing and thinking about the previous night. On the plus side, the eleven o'clock news had reported a break-in at Violet Comstock's house by "two unidentified men in their twenties." That meant neither Violet nor the reporters who'd been hanging around outside her house had gotten a good look at us, and they definitely hadn't recognized us.

On the negative side, the news of Sissy Rae's disappearance was starting to affect business. People had called steadily all evening to cancel their reservations, and most of the night the restaurant was only half full. I let out a sigh and squirted some more shampoo onto my hair. Mom and Dad had taken out a massive loan to open Baby Bistro, and they needed big crowds if they were ever going to get ahead. Instead, people were staying away in droves, and it was all because of me.

I set my jaw and scrubbed my scalp. I was determined to find Sissy Rae. I finished rinsing off, then I stepped out of the shower and checked my hair in the mirror. All right! My hair was blond again! I threw on some clothes and headed for the deck to get my bike.

"Hold on, Puck," Dad called from the kitchen. "Where are you off to?"

"Jackson's house," I called back. I didn't mention that we were planning to take a bus to Burbank so we could snoop around Pearl Pendergast's office.

"Sorry, buddy. Captain Nishio just called. He wants your mom and me to come to the station so he can ask us some more questions. We need you to baby-sit Julia."

I let out a groan and stomped into the kitchen. Mom was making blueberry pancakes while Dad squeezed fresh orange juice. Julia was on the floor, sucking down a bottle of apple juice.

"Can't you go some other time?" I pleaded. "I really want to see Jackson this morning."

"You just saw him last night," Mom pointed out. "Anyway, we don't want to be uncooperative. The sooner Captain Nishio finds the real kidnapper, the sooner our names will be cleared."

What could I say? Mom and Dad were right. Besides, how could I complain about baby-sitting Julia when they were being so nice to me? Not once since this mess started had they blamed me for allowing Sissy Rae to get covered with food, or for taking her to the bathroom without telling anyone where we were going, or even for leaving her in there alone.

"Okay," I said, forcing myself to smile. "I'll take care of the munchkin. No problem."

"Thanks, Puck," Mom said. "And make sure she doesn't have any more bottles. We've got her down to one a day."

As if on cue, Julia sucked down the last ounce of apple juice and let out an angry squeal. "Buh-boo," she cried, banging her bottle on the floor. "Want buh-boo!"

I sighed. It was going to be a long morning.

"Bus!" Julia squealed happily. "Big bus!"

I didn't bother to answer. Julia had been crowing about the "big bus" ever since Jackson and I had carried her onto it twenty minutes earlier. She'd probably still be at it when we used our transfers to board the second bus for the rest of our trip to Burbank.

Yep, Burbank. I'd planned to stay home and baby-sit Julia—really, I had—but after Mom and Dad left for the police station, Jackson had called. When I told him what was going on, he suggested we take Julia along with us to Pearl Pendergast's office. It was courting disaster, I know, but I let him talk me into it, mostly because I couldn't stand the thought of facing a morning of toddlermania alone. So there we were, rumbling up the Hollywood Freeway with Julia, Loola, and a bulging diaper bag between us on the seat.

Forty-five minutes and one totally disgusting diaper change later, we were pulling up in front of the building where Pearl Pendergast had her office. Julia had a major tantrum when she realized we were taking her away from her beloved bus, and she was still going strong when we carried her, kicking and screaming, into the lobby.

"How about a ride on the elevator?" I asked, trying to sound cheerful.

"Big bus!" she sobbed. "Want big bus!"

Men in business suits stared at us as we dragged her

toward the elevators, and a couple of women scowled as if they planned to report us for child abuse.

Jackson drummed his fingers against the elevator doors. "Open," he pleaded.

Finally, they did. I took a step inside and found myself face-to-face with Will Faraday. "Will!" I exclaimed with surprise.

He looked even more startled than I did. Then he smiled. "Hey, boys. Hey, Miss Julie."

Julia stopped screaming. "Me ride big bus!" she proclaimed.

"Good for you," Will said, reaching out to wipe a tear from her cheek. "I'll bet that was fun."

"What are you doing here, Will?" Jackson asked.

"I just applied for a job as a janitor. Not that I'm plannin' to leave the restaurant," he added quickly. "This is just a part-time job to pick up a little more cash."

"Buh-boo!" Julia exclaimed suddenly, pointing at Will.

"Knock it off, Julia," I said impatiently. "Will doesn't have a bottle for you. Anyway, Mom says you're big enough to drink out of a cup now."

"Buh-boo!" she insisted, thrusting her little finger toward the pocket of Will's overalls. "Want buh-boo!"

Will chuckled and patted her head. "Gotta run. I have three loads of laundry to do before Baby Bistro opens." He hurried out of the elevator just as the doors started to close. "See y'all tonight," he called over his shoulder.

"That guy must be Santa Claus in disguise," I said as the elevator started to rise. "Julia just has to take one look at him and she starts grinning."

"You know what's weird?" Jackson replied. "He didn't ask us what *we* were doing here."

I shrugged. "Well, he said he was in a hurry." Before I

could think about it any further, the elevator doors opened and we were gazing into the reception area of the Pearl Pendergast Talent Agency. There was a redheaded receptionist with two-inch-long black fingernails sitting behind a desk, four empty upholstered chairs, and a ten-gallon fish tank filled with tropical fish.

The receptionist glanced up at us. "Ms. Pendergast handles established stars only," she said in a bored monotone.

"What?" I asked blankly.

"We don't handle new faces," she droned. "Try Modern Talent, suite three-fourteen on the third floor."

"Oh," I said, finally getting it, "we're not looking for an agent. We're, uh . . ."

"The fish-tank boys," Jackson said. "We're here to clean out the fish tank."

"Don't think so," the receptionist replied. "The tank was just cleaned last week—by me."

I laughed weakly. "He's joking, of course. We're here to meet our father, uh, Irving Steinwald. He's having a meeting with Pearl Pendergast." Grabbing Julia's hand, I stepped out of the elevator with false confidence and headed for the hallway that led to the inner offices. "He said we should go right—"

"Freeze!" the receptionist bellowed. I obeyed, and so did Jackson. Even Julia hesitated. "If Irving Steinwald was here, I would know it," she said. "If he had three children, I would know that, too. I know *everything* that goes on around here, and I do not know you. So make like a breeze and blow before I call the security guard."

I looked into the receptionist's steel-blue eyes and knew she meant business. Apparently, talking our way into Pearl Pendergast's office wasn't going to be as easy as talking our way into Violet Comstock's house. I bit my lip and tried to think what Sam Spade, Philip Marlowe, or one of the other classic movie detectives would do in a situation like this. But before I could figure it out, the elevator doors opened and a man with a brown ponytail walked in, leading three enormous Great Danes on studded leather leashes.

"Horsies!" Julia exclaimed eagerly, toddling toward them.

"Those aren't horses," I corrected, grabbing her hand and pulling her back. "They're dogs. Big dogs."

"Good morning, Mr. Zelsner," the receptionist said. She shot us an icy look. "These children were just leaving, weren't you, kids?" She turned back to Zelsner. "Are these the dogs for the new Daring Dog Food commercial?"

"They sure are," the man replied proudly, leading them up to her desk. "Three of the best-trained dogs in the business."

Julia pulled at my hand. "Me ride horsies!"

"Come on, Julia," Jackson broke in. "Let's go." He reached down for her other hand, but she snatched it away from him and leaned longingly toward the dogs.

"The casting people should be here shortly," the receptionist said, pointedly ignoring us. "They want to see how little Bobby and Michelle look with the—"

"Ride horsies!" Julia insisted, yanking her hand out of mine and rushing toward them. She grabbed the closest dog by the tail and tried to pull herself onto its back.

The dog let out a yelp and spun around, flinging slobber everywhere. Julia squealed with fear and batted the beast on the nose. *"Rowf!"* the dog barked, straining at his leash. *"Rowf! Rowf!"*

"Duke, no!" Zelsner shouted. He turned to the receptionist, who had jumped to her feet and was heading around the desk. "Rosemary, get these kids out of . . ."

The other dogs were barking now, completely drowning out Zelsner's voice. Julia held her ears and let out a piercing shriek that was even louder than the dogs. Duke jerked away, pulling his leash out of Zelsner's hand, and took off running. He bounded over a chair and crashed into the fish tank. It toppled to the floor, splashing water, coral, fish, and a tiny sunken ship onto the carpet.

The dogs were there in a flash, eagerly gobbling up the flapping fish while Rosemary screamed and batted the Great Danes on the heads with a rolled-up magazine.

"Stop!" Zelsner cried. "Those dogs are worth a small fortune!"

"So are my fish!" she cried hysterically.

Jackson nudged me in the ribs. "This is our chance. Come on."

He picked up Julia, who had stopped shrieking and was watching the dogs slurp down the fish, and tiptoed toward the hallway. I glanced at Rosemary and Zelsner. They were much too busy shouting at the dogs and each other to care about us. Before I could change my mind, I slipped around the reception desk and followed Jackson and Julia down the hall.

Chapter

11

"Way to go, Julia," I whispered as we tiptoed down the hallway. For once my little sister's antics had been a help to me rather than an infuriating pain in the neck. I held up my hand and grinned. "Give me five, kiddo."

I don't think Julia knew what I was talking about, but she smiled up at me and slapped my hand. The expression on her face was one of pure adoration, and I realized— maybe for the first time—that she really did look up to me. It felt surprisingly good.

"In here," Jackson called softly. I glanced up to see him motioning to us from the first doorway on the left. Julia and I followed him inside and looked around.

We were in a room filled with tall, gray file cabinets. Above the cabinets were shelves lined with back issues of *Variety* and *The Hollywood Reporter*.

I closed the door and headed for the file cabinet marked *C*. Quickly, I leafed through and found Sissy Rae's file. Opening it, I found myself looking at a publicity photo of Sissy Rae's smiling face. Julia saw it and exclaimed, "Sissy Rae dance with me. Want Sissy Rae *now*!"

"Not as much as I do," I said with a sigh. I gazed at the

photo and wondered where Sissy Rae was right now. Was she scared? Sad? Maybe sick, or even hurt? *Hang in there, kid,* I said silently. *We're going to find you. I promise.*

Jackson took the file out of my hands and looked through it. "Nothing unusual in here," he said. "Just some publicity photos, a resume, some contracts, a few newspaper clippings."

"Let's keep looking around," I suggested. I peeked out into the hallway. No one was in sight. I stepped out of the room and started down the hall. Jackson and Julia followed. We'd barely walked two feet when a tall black man in slacks and a polo shirt appeared at the next doorway.

"You must be the kids for the cookie commercial," he said. "I'm Tom, Ms. Pendergast's assistant."

"Oh, uh, hi there," I said, thinking fast. "We're, uh, looking for Ms. Pendergast's office."

"Last door on the right. Hurry up. You're late."

We started down the hall, praying the man would go back inside his office. But he just kept standing there, pointing the way and smiling encouragingly. Didn't he have anything better to do? *Go back inside your office and get to work,* I thought, willing him to move.

No such luck. We were standing outside Pearl's door, the guy was still watching us, and there was nothing to do but knock. I tried to imagine what I'd say when Pearl opened the door and saw us. "Hi, remember us?" I pictured myself blurting out. "Well, er, my little sister wants to get into show business, so I brought her to meet you. She's got real charisma, don't you think?" I glanced down at Julia. Her hair was tangled, her face was dirty, and she was picking her nose. Oh, yeah, real charisma.

Jackson knocked weakly on Pearl's door. At that moment, the man stepped back inside his office. "Hide!"

Jackson hissed, darting across the hall and running through an open door.

I followed, dragging Julia with me, and closed the door behind me. "Dark," Julia announced. She was right. It was pitch-black. I felt for the light, but all I found was Jackson's nose. We both gasped and jumped back, then burst out laughing.

Suddenly, the door opened and the room was flooded with light. We blinked, squinted—and stopped laughing. Pearl Pendergast was standing there, giving us the evil eye.

"Uh . . . uh . . . hi there," Jackson squeaked.

"What are you kids doing in my bathroom?" she demanded in her gravelly voice.

I looked around. Yep, it was the bathroom all right, and we were crowded into it like a bunch of stowaways on an ocean liner. "Uh . . . uh . . ." I gasped.

"Hey," she said, looking more closely, "you're the kids from Baby Bistro, aren't you?"

"Tha-that's right," I stuttered. "You see, my little sister wants to get into show business so, uh, I brought her here to meet you. She's got real, er, charisma, don't you think?"

Pearl glanced at Julia for maybe a microsecond. "Now tell me why you're *really* here," she snapped. "Come on, kids, spill the beans."

"Did you take a good look at that note the cops found in the restroom after Sissy Rae vanished?" Jackson said boldly. "The handwriting on it was yours."

"Mine?" Pearl frowned. "Don't be ridiculous."

"You don't believe us?" I said, trying to imitate the hard-boiled detectives I'd seen in the videos. "Why don't you call Captain Nishio and ask him to bring over the note? Then you can see for yourself."

Pearl stared at us, possibly trying to decide if we were

making the whole thing up. Then she grabbed Jackson and me by our collars and growled, "Come into my office, boys."

We followed. I mean, did we have a choice? Julia clutched my hand and toddled along. There were some toys on the floor—for the child actors to play with, I figured—and she plopped down to check them out.

"So, you boys are playing detective, huh?" Pearl asked, lighting a cigarette as she took a seat behind her desk.

"We're not playing," Jackson replied. "We're going to clear Puck's name and bring the crowds back to Baby Bistro."

"And you think I kidnapped Sissy Rae." She chuckled, then took a long drag on her cigarette and sneered at us. "Well, tell me, boys, what's my motive?"

"At first, we thought Sissy Rae's mother had kidnapped her to stir up publicity for her daughter's new TV show," I said. "But maybe you did it instead."

"Who knows?" Jackson added. "Maybe you and Violet are working together. You both treat Sissy Rae like a toddler-sized paycheck."

"Watch your mouths, boys," Pearl growled. "I've been an agent for over thirty years and no one has ever accused me of any wrongdoing." She stood up and took another drag of her cigarette. It seemed to calm her. "It's been quite amusing talking to you," she said, "but I've got a lot of work to do. I'm afraid I'm going to have to ask you to—"

"Buh-boo!" Julia exclaimed suddenly.

I jumped up and looked around. Julia had crawled behind Pearl's desk and was sitting in the corner, sucking happily on a bottle. "Where did you get that?" I demanded, rushing over to pick her up.

"In dere," she said, pointing at a pink-and-white diaper bag that was lying on the floor next to Pearl's desk. The name SISSY RAE was embroidered across the front in pink thread.

"What's that doing here?" Jackson asked.

Pearl looked completely flustered. "I . . . I have no idea," she stammered. Then she recovered. She jammed her cigarette butt into her ashtray so hard it crumpled like scrap metal in a car crusher. "I didn't kidnap Sissy Rae and you can't prove I did," she barked. "Now take a hike before I call the security guard."

"Come on, Puck," Jackson said. "Let's go to the police station and talk to Captain Nishio."

I nodded. But as I reached for the doorknob, the door swung open and a tall silver-haired man with piercing blue eyes and a lantern jaw walked in. "Ah, these must be the boys for my new Calhoun's Kooky Cookie commercial!" he exclaimed.

"No, no, Mr. Calhoun," Pearl protested. "They're—"

"They're perfect!" he went on, ignoring her. "Normally, I hate child actors, but these boys look like real kids."

"That's because we are," I explained.

"Wonderful. I'm looking for authenticity—providing you like Calhoun's Kooky Cookies, that is. But then, who doesn't?"

"Cookie!" Julia whined. "Want cookie!"

Mr. Calhoun laughed heartily. "That's what I like to hear. But I thought we decided on two boys for the commercial," he said, turning to Pearl. "What's the little girl doing here?"

"Mr. Calhoun, these are *not* the actors for your commercial," Pearl said, walking around the desk. "In fact, they're juvenile delinquents from the local detention hall. I tutor them once a week. I like to give something back to the community, you know."

Mr. Calhoun frowned and took a step backward. "Well, well, isn't that nice," he muttered uncomfortably. "Uh, so long, children. Good luck to you."

Before we could respond, Pearl grabbed Jackson and me by our elbows and dragged us out into the hallway. Julia was still in my arms, chug-a-lugging Sissy Rae's bottle.

"Bye-bye, kids," Pearl said sweetly, just loud enough for Mr. Calhoun to hear. "Don't forget to do your homework." Then she added under her breath, "If I catch you two snooping around my office again, you'll find out why Hollywood calls me the Dragon Lady. Now get lost!"

With that, she snatched the bottle out of Julia's mouth, stomped back into her office, and slammed the door.

"Okay, fellas," Captain Nishio said, escorting us into his office later that day, "here we are." He sat down at his cluttered desk and gazed at us with an *I've heard it all before* expression on his face. "Now what's the big news you want to tell me?"

I sat down in one of the straight-backed metal chairs and looked around. Nishio's office was small and cramped, with a scuffed linoleum floor and a Los Angeles Police Department calendar hanging on the dingy green wall.

"You know the handwriting on Sissy Rae's kidnapping note?" Jackson asked, taking a seat beside me. "Well, we saw Pearl Pendergast's handwriting, and it matches perfectly."

Nishio smiled indulgently. "Good job, boys. Only I figured that out the morning after the kidnapping."

"Then why haven't you arrested her?" I asked.

"Same reason I haven't arrested you. The only evidence we have is circumstantial. It's just not enough to charge Pearl Pendergast—or anyone—with kidnapping."

"But there's more," Jackson broke in. "We went to Pearl's office, and guess what we found beside her desk?"

"Sissy Rae's diaper bag?" he asked.

"How did you know?" I cried.

"I got an anonymous phone call less than an hour ago tipping me off. A woman's voice. She hung up before we could trace the call."

"It was probably one of Violet Comstock's employees," Jackson said. "Maybe Consuela, her cleaning lady. If you ask me, Violet and Pearl are in this together."

Nishio shuffled a pile of papers and placed a glass paperweight on top of them. "Possibly. But I've had my men following Pearl and Violet ever since the night of the kidnapping, and so far they haven't discovered anything incriminating."

I stared at him. "Are the police following everyone who was in the restaurant the night Sissy Rae disappeared?" I asked with surprise.

"Not exactly," he replied vaguely. "We're keeping an eye on them. Let's just leave it at that."

"I don't want to leave it at that," I said, my voice rising. "Are you telling me you've been following Jackson and me? And my parents, too?"

"Why are you so alarmed?" he asked mildly. "Do you have something to hide?"

"Of course he doesn't!" Jackson shot back. "Neither of us do. I just don't think it's right for you to be spying on us."

"Oh?" Nishio asked. "And what do you think you two have been doing? You sneaked into Violet Comstock's house, and you snooped through Pearl Pendergast's private files. I'd call that spying, wouldn't you?"

"How do you know about that stuff?" I cried.

Nishio smiled. "Like I said, we've been keeping an eye

on everyone connected with the case." He stood up and walked to the door. "If you learn anything else, don't hesitate to call me. Meanwhile, don't do anything I wouldn't do."

I walked out of the police station feeling shaky. Captain Nishio knew everything we knew, possibly lots more. But what really threw me was the realization that he and his men had been following Jackson and me for days, watching our every move. In fact, they were probably spying on us right now.

I spun around, half-expecting to see a guy in a trench coat and a crumpled fedora stalking me. But no one was there.

"Forget it, Puck," Jackson said, reading my mind. "They're much more clever than that." He pointed to some city workers who were opening a manhole cover in the sidewalk. "It could be them. Or them." He motioned toward some middle-aged women carrying shopping bags.

"Stop it," I said. "You're making me paranoid."

"Sorry," he replied as we unlocked our bikes from the rack. We climbed on and hit the road. "It's not the fact that Nishio is having us followed that bothers me," Jackson said after a block or two. "It's the fact that he's about ten steps ahead of us and he *still* doesn't have a clue who kidnapped Sissy Rae."

"Or why," I added.

"Or even if she's still alive."

I pedaled another few blocks, my mind seething with all sorts of horrible fantasies about what might have happened to Sissy Rae. And then I thought of something that *really* freaked me out. If the cops were watching us, maybe Sissy Rae's kidnapper was too. And maybe it wasn't Violet or Pearl, but some total wacko who didn't like the fact that we were snooping around, trying to figure out who he was. And maybe, just maybe, if we found out too much, he'd decide to kidnap us, too.

"You know, Jackson, I've been thinking," I said anxiously. "Maybe we ought to leave the investigating to the police. I mean, after all, they're the pro—"

I never finished the sentence. At that moment a beat-up black pickup truck that was traveling down the other side of the street veered across the yellow line and screeched toward us. "Look out!" I screamed, throwing down my bike and flinging myself at the curb. Jackson ditched his bike and leaped after me. We both landed in a heap in the gutter.

The pickup skidded to a halt facing the wrong way. I looked up, heart pounding and hands shaking. The truck's tailgate was facing us. I couldn't see the driver, but as I staggered to my feet I heard a gruff voice warn, "Stop looking for Sissy Rae, or you'll be sorry!" Then, with a squeal of burning rubber, the pickup roared back to the right side of the road and drove away.

Chapter
12

"Zoom! Zoom!"

Julia's whiny voice cut through my consciousness like a chainsaw through concrete. I rolled over and squinted at my bedside clock. Six A.M.

I let out a groan and pulled the pillow over my head. My brain felt like lumpy oatmeal, and my body wasn't much better. That was because I'd spent the night having nightmares about Sissy Rae's kidnapper and the fiendish things he was planning to do to me. In one dream, he looked like Mr. Calhoun, the Kooky Cookie man, and he was forcing me to eat an entire truckload of stale cookies—without milk. In another, the kidnapper was Violet Comstock, and she was pouring chlorine on my hair, turning it a permanently hideous shade of lime-green.

But then I thought back to the day before, and my nightmares seemed like pleasant daydreams compared with what had really happened. I could still see that black pickup truck tearing toward me and smell the burning rubber as it sped away. Even worse, the driver's words were still ringing in my ears. "Stop looking for Sissy Rae, or you'll be sorry!"

Naturally, after checking to make sure our bodies and our bikes were still in one piece, Jackson and I had hurried back to Captain Nishio's office to tell him what had happened. Unfortunately, our story was kind of sketchy. Neither of us had gotten a look at the driver, and we'd been too stunned to notice the truck's license plate. We hadn't recognized the driver's voice either. In fact, we weren't even sure if it belonged to a man or a woman.

Captain Nishio wrote down everything we told him, but he wasn't exactly reassuring. I mean, I was expecting him to assign a couple dozen cops to guard Jackson and me twenty-four hours a day until the kidnapper was captured. At the very least, I figured he'd remove my name from the list of suspects. Instead, all he said was, "Don't go anywhere without your parents, and let me know if you hear from the kidnapper again."

"Zoom! Zoom!"

My thoughts were cut short when the bedroom door flew open and Julia rolled in, pushing herself on her plastic tricycle. She had my bike helmet perched on her head, and her tiny hands were hidden inside my leather racing gloves.

"See, Uck?" she cooed happily. "Me ride bike, too!"

She looked so cute and funny, I had to smile. And then I realized something. Lately, Julia and I had been getting along a lot better. To my amazement, I only wanted to strangle her once or twice a day instead of every fifteen seconds.

The reason was Will Faraday. He had a way with kids, and ever since he'd started working at the restaurant, he'd been giving me tips on how to handle Julia. For example, a few nights before, I had told him how Julia was always coming into my room and messing up my stuff. He told me she'd be just as happy to clean up my room as she would to destroy it—*if* I made the whole thing seem like a game.

It seemed hard to believe, but Will hadn't steered me wrong so far. Anyway, I needed to do something to get my mind off yesterday. So I decided to try it. "You look good riding that bike, Julia," I said, throwing my legs over the side of my bed. "Just like a big kid." She beamed. "Now how'd you like to play a big kid game with me?"

She nodded eagerly. "Game with Uck."

"Okay. This game is called the Pick-up Game. See all that stuff on the floor?" I asked, pointing to the piles of dirty clothes, shoes, mountain biking magazines, pencils, scraps of paper, candy bar wrappers, and other assorted junk. "Well, I'm going to sing a song, and you're going to listen and do what I tell you. You think you're a big enough girl to do that?"

"Me *very* big," she answered.

"Okay, let's try it." I threw back my head and broke into an off-key rendition of the song Will had taught me. "Pick it up, pick it up, pick up the T-shirt. Pick it up, pick it up, put it in the hamper." I stopped singing and asked, "Can you do that, Julia?"

Julia looked around the room and spotted my dirty T-shirt. Eagerly she picked it up and shoved it into the hamper.

"Good job!" I exclaimed. "Now try this one. Pick it up, pick it up, pick up the pencil. Pick it up, pick it up, put it in my desk."

Within seconds, she had found the pencil and put it in my desk drawer. "Again," she demanded. "Uck sing!"

She didn't have to ask twice. I sang verse after verse, and Julia kept picking things up. Within minutes, she had straightened my entire room. She'd even enjoyed it. Come to think of it, I had, too.

I was just about to send Julia under my bed to search for my missing bike pump when the doorbell rang. Of course, my first thought was that it was the kidnapper returning to finish what he (she?) had started yesterday. My insides churned as I imagined opening the front door and seeing a black pickup truck barreling toward me at top speed.

I guess Mom and Dad were thinking the same thing, because when they stumbled into the hallway, hair mussed and still wearing their pajamas, they looked pretty stressed. "Don't open the door, Puck," Dad warned, walking to the window and peering out. "Stay back, and keep Julia with you."

"If it's a stranger, don't answer it," Mom called.

But it wasn't a stranger. It was Captain Nishio. "I'm very sorry to disturb you so early in the morning, but I thought you'd want to see this," he said, holding up a plastic bag with a crumpled piece of paper inside it. "Someone left it on Violet Comstock's front steps. Her newspaper boy found it when he delivered her morning paper, and she immediately contacted me."

He handed my father the bag containing the paper. It was another message, a combination of handwritten words and pasted-on letters. SISSY RAE IS HAPPY AND HEALTHY, it read. STOP LOOKING FOR HER.

Mom took one look and gasped. "That handwriting . . ." she began.

"It's . . . it's mine," Dad said incredulously.

At that moment a flashbulb went off, half-blinding us. A reporter leaped out of the bushes next to our front walk and thrust a tape recorder at my father. "Any comment you'd like to make to the press?" he asked.

"Hold it right there!" Captain Nishio commanded,

displaying his police badge to the reporter. "You're under arrest for trespassing."

The guy didn't even flinch. He just ran off down the sidewalk and jumped into a waiting van at the end of the street. It was too far away to make out the license plate, and within seconds the van had screeched away.

Dad turned to Captain Nishio and shoved the plastic bag into his hands. "I didn't send this letter," he said forcefully. "And I didn't kidnap Sissy Rae."

"I'd like to believe you," Nishio answered. He sounded sincere.

"Thanks," Mom said glumly, "but after that reporter sells his story, I doubt the public will. We'll be lucky if the restaurant is half full tonight."

Dad nodded, suddenly subdued. "It was fun while it lasted," he said, putting his arm around Mom's shoulder, "but I'm afraid it's time to kiss Baby Bistro good-bye."

"You want to sing a chorus of 'Greasy, Grimy Gopher Guts'?" Jackson asked.

"Why bother?" I replied, watching as the only two toddlers in Baby Bistro—a set of one-year-old twins— gummed their breadsticks. I let out a sigh. Back when business was booming, I would have given anything to be able to kick back and relax for a few minutes, but now it was downright depressing.

Dad walked in from the foyer. His welcoming maitre d' smile had been replaced by a worried frown. "This place feels more like a morgue than a baby restaurant," he remarked, looking around.

"It's only six o'clock," I said. "Maybe things will pick up."

"Don't bet on it. Everyone with a reservation has

111

canceled. All we can hope for is a few walk-in customers."

"People couldn't get in here even if they wanted to," Jackson said, peering out the window. "There must be fifteen reporters and photographers out front, plus a couple of guys with video cameras."

"Those vultures!" Dad muttered, shaking his fist. "It's because of them and their lies that the restaurant is doing so badly."

The morning papers had trumpeted the news that my father's handwriting had been found on the latest kidnapping note. One paper had even included a photo of Violet Comstock with the quote "I wish I'd never set foot in Baby Bistro." After all that, it wasn't surprising that people were staying away.

"It's not the media's fault," I said. "It's mine. If I hadn't left Sissy Rae alone in the bathroom, none of this would have happened."

"Stop beating yourself up, Puck," Dad said, putting on a brave smile. "To tell you the truth, I was getting tired of running my own restaurant. After the cops find the real kidnapper and all this blows over, I'm going to find a job in a nice, quiet pizza parlor."

I knew Dad was lying, but I didn't contradict him. What was the point? I glanced over at the twins. They were cheerfully smearing chocolate pudding in each other's hair. "I guess we'd better clean them up," I said half-heartedly, turning to Jackson.

"Go to it, boys," Dad said. "I'll see how things are going in the kitchen."

Jackson and I separated the twins and distracted them by spinning a top that plays "Old MacDonald." Then I left Jackson to clean the pudding out of their hair, and followed Dad into the kitchen.

I found Will at the stove. Julia was standing on a stepstool beside him. They were pouring herbs and spices into a big pot of water, and Julia was stirring the concoction with a long wooden spoon.

"What are you making?" I asked.

"Dis 'n' dat stew," Julia replied, as if everyone in the world knew what she was talking about.

I looked at Will questioningly. "We put in a little of this and a little of that," he explained with a grin. "You wanna taste it, Puck?"

I wrinkled my nose. "I think I'll pass. Where are Mom and Dad?"

Will motioned toward the back door. I walked into the alley and found them leaning against the wall near where Jackson and I had parked our bikes, talking in low, serious voices. ". . . cut our losses and put it on the market," Dad was saying.

Mom looked stricken. "But it could be months before we find a buyer. What about our loan payments? And our mortgage is due next week."

Just then, Dad looked up and saw me. "Puck!" he exclaimed with fake enthusiasm. "We were just going inside, weren't we, Sandy?"

"That's right," Mom said, tousling my hair as she walked by.

I followed them back into the kitchen. My chest felt heavy, like there was a bowling ball inside it. I didn't understand everything my parents had been talking about, but I knew it was bad.

Jackson was waiting for us. "The twins' parents paid and left," he announced. "The restaurant's empty."

Dad frowned. "I'll send the waiters and busboys home. No point paying them to stand around."

"Before you go, can I talk to you?" Will asked, stepping forward.

"Why, sure, Will," Dad replied. "What is it?"

"Well, I hate to have to say this, but I've decided to move on."

"Move on?" Mom asked. "What do you mean?"

"I'm homesick for Iowa and I'm going back," he explained.

"You mean you're leaving?" I cried.

Will nodded. "I'm gonna miss you folks. We haven't known each other long, but I kinda feel like we're family."

I knew exactly what he meant. Will fit in so well at the restaurant, it was almost as if he were a long-lost relative instead of a mere employee. I gazed up into his friendly, basset-hound eyes and felt a lump forming in my throat. I didn't want Will to leave. I was really going to miss him.

Dad shook his head. "Gosh, Will, I wish I could offer you a big raise and beg you to stay," he said sadly, "but I can't. The restaurant has been losing money ever since Sissy Rae disappeared, and unless a miracle happens, we'll be closing at the end of the week."

I guess I'd suspected it all along, but hearing Dad say it made my heart sink. Baby Bistro was closing, and my parents' dream of owning their own restaurant was over. I looked around the kitchen. Everyone seemed about ready to cry. Even Julia, who didn't fully understand what was going on, looked heartbroken.

"Let's close up," Mom said with a sigh. "I doubt we'll be seeing any more customers tonight. Besides, I'm too depressed to cook."

Dad went into the office and wrote Will a check for his last few days of work. "Hope this doesn't bounce," he said with a hollow laugh, handing it to him.

Will took it and shook my father's hand. Then he gave us each a hug. "So long, y'all," he said, putting on his jacket. "I can't thank you enough for everything you've done for me. And as far as the restaurant goes—well, I'm sorry as can be. Really I am. I wish things could have worked out differently, but, well, I just had to—"

"Buh-boo!" Julia cried suddenly, pointing up at him.

We all looked at her with irritation. How could she be thinking about bottles at a time like this? But Will just laughed. "You're a big girl now, Julia," he said, kneeling down to pat her head. "You can drink from a cup, just like Puck." He kissed her cheek and smiled. Then he stood up, gave us all a little wave, and walked out the back door.

"Buh-boo," Julia said again.

"Julia, be quiet," I snapped. "Can't you see we're all . . ." My voice trailed off as I noticed she was pointing to something. I walked over and looked. There was a small puddle of white liquid on the floor right where Will had been kneeling.

"Jackson," I said, "check this out. Does this look like milk to you?"

"I guess," he replied. "So what?" Then slowly, his eyes widened. "You don't think—?"

"—that Will really did have a bottle in his pocket?" I said. "Yes, I do."

"But why?" Mom asked, coming over to see for herself. "He doesn't have a baby."

"So he says," I agreed. "But then he also told us he comes from Arkansas. So how come he's suddenly homesick for Iowa?"

"Iowa?" Dad repeated thoughtfully. "Didn't I recently read about someone who was born in Iowa?"

"You sure did," Jackson exclaimed. "Sissy Rae Comstock!"

"Come on!" I cried, grabbing Jackson's sleeve as I headed for the back door. "We've got to stop Will before he gets away!"

Chapter
13

Jackson and I ran out the back door and looked up and down the alley, but Will was nowhere in sight. "You go left, I'll go right," I said.

Jackson ran toward Sixth Street while I headed for Fifth Street. I got to the corner just in time to see a black pickup truck—just like the one that had tried to run us over—pulling away from the curb. The back was piled high with luggage, a stroller, a crib, and a rocking horse.

I sprinted down the sidewalk, hoping to catch a glimpse of the driver. My view was blocked by the woman sitting in the passenger seat. She was about sixty, with a well-lined face and black hair teased into a huge bouffant.

The woman must have spotted me out of the corner of her eye, because she turned toward me. For a brief moment, I got a look at the driver. It was Will Faraday.

"Will!" I shouted, but it was too late. The pickup changed lanes and disappeared into the dense traffic.

I turned and ran back to the restaurant. Jackson had returned and was talking to my mother, father, and sister. When I burst through the door, they all looked up. "I saw him," I said breathlessly. "He's in the black pickup with some lady, and there's a bunch of baby stuff in the back. They're heading down Fifth Street toward Broadway."

"Did they have Sissy Rae with them?" Mom asked.

"I couldn't tell. I only saw them for a few seconds. I shouted at Will but he drove away."

"I'll call Captain Nishio," Dad said, reaching for the phone.

Jackson turned to me. "It's rush hour," he said impatiently. "We'll be lucky if he gets here in less than thirty minutes."

"Longer. You'd need a motorcycle to get through that traffic. Even a bike would be better than . . ." My voice trailed off as I realized what I'd just said.

"You up for it?" Jackson asked.

I nodded, my heart racing in anticipation. "Let's go!"

We ran out the back door and unlocked our bikes. My mother ran after us. "Where are you going?" she demanded.

"To stop Will and find Sissy Rae," I said.

"In this traffic?" Mom cried, shaking her head. "It's much too dangerous. Come back inside and wait for the—"

"Sissy Rae," Julia whined, toddling out the back door with Loola in her arms. "Want Sissy Rae."

Mom leaned down to pick her up. Jackson hopped on his bike and pedaled past her, heading up the alley toward Fifth Street. "Jackson, wait!" Mom shouted. "Puck, don't—"

But I couldn't let Jackson go without me. Besides, the way my adrenaline was pumping, I don't think the National Guard could have stopped me. "Don't worry. We know what we're doing," I lied. Then I took off up the alley after Jackson.

Fifth Street was packed with cars, all of them exceeding the speed limit. People were cutting each other off, speeding up and then slamming on their brakes when the car ahead of them stopped. Jackson swerved in front of a hesitating driver and took off down the center line, pedaling hard. I followed him. Halfway down the block, we caught sight of the black pickup.

Drivers were honking at us, but we didn't care. We stood up and pedaled harder. The pickup was boxed in by the heavy traffic, and soon we were coasting up beside it. Now I could see the car seat strapped in between the two adults and the little red-headed girl who was sitting in it.

"Sissy Rae!" I shouted.

The lady with the big hair snapped her head around. When she saw me, her jaw dropped. "It's them kids!" she cried. She turned to Will. "Step on it, Sonny!"

Will hit the accelerator. The pickup jerked forward, but there was nowhere for it to go. The car in front of it was slowing down, anticipating the red light up ahead. Then Will spotted a break in the oncoming traffic and cut left—right across the double yellow line! He passed the two cars that were blocking his way, swerved back into his lane, and barreled through the red light, leaving us far behind.

"Follow me!" I shouted to Jackson. I hopped the curb and pedaled up the crowded sidewalk. Businessmen and shoppers screamed and leaped out of the way as we raced toward the intersection. Up ahead, the traffic light was turning green. I shifted into a higher gear and tore into the intersection. That's when I saw the orange traffic cones, the pile of dirt, and the city worker climbing out of the open manhole in the middle of the street.

My brain froze. A microsecond later, it switched back on and I knew what I had to do. I hit the pile of dirt at high speed, blasted off the top, and sailed over the manhole, missing the worker by mere inches.

When my wheels touched asphalt again, I was grinning from ear to ear. Talk about incredible! I'd just pulled off the hottest mountain biking maneuver of my life. But there was no time to congratulate myself. I was skidding down the wrong side of the street and there was a huge truck heading my way!

The truck driver hit his horn and slammed on his brakes, and I swerved back to the center of the street. Breathing hard, I glanced over my shoulder. Jackson had survived the leap over the manhole and was pedaling up behind me. I allowed myself a relieved sigh, then turned my attention to the traffic ahead. The black pickup was half a block ahead of us, turning onto Sixth Street. I followed, and by the time we were halfway up Sixth, I was right behind it.

Pershing Square, a block-long plaza with a reflecting pool and an enormous fountain, lay ahead. This time I saw the traffic cones. They were spread out across the full width of the street, along with a big orange arrow with the word DETOUR on it. Beyond the cones, a fleet of trucks and motor homes was parked along the edge of the square. I could see a group of people scurrying around the fountain, carrying lights and equipment.

I knew immediately what was going on. A movie crew was filming on location—a common sight in L.A. But Will either didn't realize what was happening or didn't care. Ignoring the detour sign, he burst through the traffic cones, skidded right, and bumped up onto the sidewalk. Then he downshifted and rattled up the wide concrete stairs that led into the park.

By now, Jackson had caught up with me. "Follow him!" he cried. We stood up on our bikes and pedaled with all our might. Side by side, we bounced up the stairs and followed the pickup across the open plaza. The movie crew scattered, dropping expensive lights and sound equipment as they leaped out of our way. The pickup plowed into a camera and kept going. I swerved to miss a man who was running across the park. Hey, was that Tom Cruise?

But there was no time for a second look. The pickup had roared out of the square and was heading up Olive Street. We pedaled after it, dodging traffic to keep up. Behind us I heard police sirens. The pickup turned right down the steep Fourth Street hill, then moved into the left lane to make the turn onto Hill Street.

"Shortcut!" I shouted, pointing to the grassy hillside that stretched from Olive Street down to Hill. But Jackson already had the same idea. He was halfway across the street, cutting in front of a delivery van as he pedaled toward the curb.

I followed. Together we skidded across the sidewalk and barreled down the embankment. Out of the corner of my eye, I could see Angels Flight, the little railway that carries pedestrians and tourists up and down Bunker Hill. The people in the cable cars were leaning out the windows, pointing at us. Then suddenly, I noticed something orange and brown lying in the grass. It was a sleeping homeless person, and if I didn't do something fast, I was going to hit him!

I swerved right, then cut left to avoid a rock. My bike's front end wobbled, just as it always did during tight cutbacks, and I lost my balance. Wipeout!

I hit the grass and started to roll. When I stopped, Jackson was standing over me. He grabbed my hand and dragged me to my feet.

"Look at me," I moaned, gazing down at my shredded knees. "I'm a mess!"

"We'll deal with that later," he said, pointing over my

shoulder. "Right now we've got something bigger to worry about."

I spun around. Two grim-looking cops had parked their motorcycles at the curb and were striding toward us. "Oh, great," I muttered. "They're probably going to arrest us for breaking through that roadblock and disrupting the movie set."

"By the time we explain what's going on, Will and Sissy Rae will be long gone," Jackson said impatiently.

I looked at him. He looked back at me. I knew we were thinking the same thing. Without a word, we picked up our bikes and hopped on.

"Hey, where do you kids think you're going?" the cops shouted, breaking into a run. "Stop! *Stop!*"

Ignoring my throbbing knees, I took off down the hill. Jackson was right behind me. We coasted across the sidewalk and into the street just as the black pickup turned the corner.

Now what? We had to find a way to make Will stop. But how? Suddenly I had an idea. With my heart pounding, I pedaled up behind the pickup and grabbed the tailgate. The junk piled in the back blocked the rear window, so I was pretty sure Will and Big Hair couldn't see me. Then I ditched my bike and jumped into the truck bed.

Rush hour was ending and the traffic was thinning out. Will stepped on the gas and the pickup lurched forward. I grabbed Sissy Rae's crib and hung on for dear life. When my heart finally returned to something resembling normal, I looked behind me, expecting to see Jackson pedaling after us. But he was gone.

My stomach churned. Had he been hit by a car? I stood on tiptoe, scanning the traffic. Then I spotted him. The motorcycle cops had pulled him over near the entrance to

Angels Flight. They stood on either side of him, grasping his arms while he twisted and turned like a bug in a spiderweb.

It was all up to me now. I took a deep breath and began to make my way toward the cab of the pickup truck. I felt like a rock climber, precariously pulling myself over suitcases and boxes, baby equipment and toys.

Finally, I reached the cab. Shoving aside a changing table, I knocked on the rear window. Sissy Rae twisted in her car seat. When she saw me, she squealed with delight. But Big Hair wasn't so welcoming. She let out a gasp, then scowled and tapped Will's shoulder.

He glanced behind him. When he saw me, his mouth fell open. "Get off, Puck!" he shouted, rolling down his window. "You're going to get hurt up there."

"I'm not getting off until you stop this truck and hand over Sissy Rae," I called.

"I can't do that," he called back. "Now listen to me, Puck. I'm gonna slow down and I want you to jump off."

Will downshifted, but instead of jumping off, I grabbed the nearest suitcase—a pink-flowered one that felt like it was filled with ball bearings—and heaved it over the roof of the cab. It landed on the front windshield, obscuring Will's view.

"Darn it, Puck!" he shouted, slamming on the brakes. "I'm trying to help Sissy Rae, not hurt her. Now get off the truck or I'll—"

A siren split the air, drowning out Will's voice. I spun around, expecting to see the motorcycle cops. Instead I saw a black-and-white police car about half a block behind us. A plainclothes cop stuck his head out the passenger window. It was Captain Nishio!

"Stop the truck!" he shouted through a megaphone. "Turn off the engine and step out with your hands in the—"

Big Hair didn't wait to hear the rest. She reached out the

123

window, grabbed the suitcase, and flung it into the street. "Step on it, Sonny!" she ordered.

"Hold on, Puck!" Will warned. He put the pedal to the metal and we flew forward, swerving onto the curb to pass a line of slow-moving cars. I clutched the side of the truck bed as we swung onto Third Street and barreled up the hill. We shot through a red light at Olive Street, then turned onto Grand Avenue, sideswiping a couple of parked cars in the process.

Will turned right at Fifth Street, and I knew he was heading for the on-ramp to the Harbor Freeway. I crouched in the back of the truck, my legs shaking like strands of wet spaghetti, praying I wouldn't fly off.

And then I saw something that made my heart leap. It was a hunched-over figure on a mountain bike pedaling furiously into the intersection. I leaned forward to get a better look. It was Jackson!

I couldn't imagine how he'd convinced the motorcycle cops to let him go, but I wasn't complaining. I scrambled to my feet and waved my arms. "Jackson!" I screamed. "Over here!"

He saw me and pedaled harder. I grabbed Sissy Rae's stroller and flung it over the roof onto the truck's windshield, hoping to slow Will down. He swerved right, and the pickup skidded against a parked car. The impact threw me sideways into Sissy Rae's rocking horse.

As I staggered to my feet, I found myself gazing at the tile-covered tower of the Los Angeles Public Library. Up at the end of the block, a librarian was emptying books from a curbside book-return box and loading them into a cart. As I watched her, a desperate idea popped into my brain. It was a long shot, but it was better than nothing.

"Jackson!" I screamed, pointing toward the librarian. "Hit the cart! Hit the cart!"

Jackson stared at me blankly. Then he spotted the book cart and his eyes lit up. Leaning over the handlebars, he pedaled like a demon toward the librarian. "Move!" he bellowed. "Get out of the way!"

The librarian took one look at Jackson charging toward her and let out a shriek that could be heard in the next county. Then she turned and ran. An instant later, Jackson's front wheel collided with the book cart. Talk about perfect timing! The cart skidded into the street, books flying everywhere, and toppled over right in front of the speeding pickup.

Will hit the brakes. The book cart jammed beneath his front bumper. The pickup skidded to the right, bounced up over the curb, and plowed into a fire hydrant. There was a moment of silence and then a loud gushing sound. Suddenly an enormous torrent of water shot into the air. It fell on the truck, drenching the suitcases, the boxes, the toys, and me.

I jumped out of the truck as the motorcycle cops roared up behind us, sirens wailing. A moment later, Captain Nishio's patrol car appeared. Ignoring them all, I ran to the front of the pickup and flung open the door. Jackson ran around to the other side and did the same.

"Puck," Will began, climbing out, "let me explain . . ."

But I was focused on Sissy Rae. I leaned across the seat to look at her. Believe it or not, she was fast asleep, a pink pacifier resting between her pouty lips. I reached down to unbuckle her car seat, but Big Hair grabbed a copy of *Elmo's ABCs* and whacked me on the head. Jackson reached for the book. She lunged at him, missed, and fell out of the truck onto the flooded sidewalk.

I took advantage of the distraction to free Sissy Rae. As I lifted her out of the truck, she woke up and gazed groggily at Will. I expected her to burst into tears. Instead, she held out her arms to him and whimpered, "I want my daddy!"

Chapter

14

"Daddy?" I gasped, dumbfounded.

Will smiled sheepishly and reached for Sissy Rae. She practically leaped into his arms. "I'm Sissy Rae's father," he said, walking down the sidewalk to escape the geyser of water from the broken fire hydrant.

"But . . . but . . ." Jackson stammered, appearing around the side of the truck. "I thought Sissy Rae's father was dead."

Before Will could answer, the two motorcycle cops ran up and snapped handcuffs on Jackson and me. "You're under arrest," announced the cop who was clutching my arm. "You have the right to remain silent. Anything you say can and will—"

"Hold on, officers," Will broke in. "These boys haven't done anything wrong. They were just tryin' to protect Sissy Rae."

"He's right," Captain Nishio said, strolling toward us with two uniformed officers, one male, one female. "Take the handcuffs off the kids. This man and lady are the ones to be arrested." He pointed to Big Hair, who was sitting on the sidewalk, her formerly puffy hair hanging limply around her face. "They're both wanted for kidnapping."

The bewildered motorcycle cops took off our handcuffs, while the other officers snapped their own sets of cuffs on Will and Big Hair. Jackson headed across the street in the direction of the book-return box.

"Where do you think you're going?" Nishio asked.

"My bike—" Jackson began, but the captain cut him off.

"Just because you're not in handcuffs doesn't mean you're free to go," he said. "I want you to come to the station and answer a few questions. Your bikes will be picked up and held as evidence." He turned to me. "We'll have one of the paramedics from the fire department stop by the station to check out those cuts. They look nasty."

I glanced down at my bloody knees. In all the excitement, I had completely forgotten about them. "It's no big deal," I said.

Nishio shook his head. "You boys are brave, but you've got the common sense of seaweed. You could have been killed cycling through that traffic. Now get in the patrol car."

Will and Big Hair were already inside, sitting in the backseat. We slid in beside them. Will gazed longingly out the window at Sissy Rae, who was sobbing in the arms of the female police officer. "Where are you takin' her?" he asked Nishio, who was getting into the driver's seat. "You're not givin' her back to her mama, are you?"

"Can you give me one good reason why I shouldn't?" the captain asked, starting the car.

"Yes, sir, I can. After our divorce, the court awarded Violet and me joint custody of Sissy Rae. We were both supposed to stay in Iowa, but about six months ago Violet took Sissy Rae and hightailed it across the state line in the middle of the night." He looked at Nishio with pleading eyes. "So you see, the real kidnapper is Violet. I was just trying to take Sissy Rae home where she belongs."

Captain Nishio thought it over. "So Violet came to Hollywood to get Sissy Rae into show business?" he asked.

Will nodded. "She'd always dreamed of an acting career for herself, and when that didn't pan out, she tried to make it happen for Sissy Rae. But I wouldn't go for it. I wanted my little girl to have a normal childhood, with time to play and lots of friends her own age. Violet knew that. That's why we got divorced in the first place."

Big Hair, who had been silent until now, suddenly piped up. "I told you that woman was trouble the first time I met her," she grumbled. "What you need is a nice down-home Arkansas gal, not some star-struck hussy from Iowa." She sighed loudly. "I don't know why on earth you married her, Sonny."

I stared at the two of them, trying to make sense of what I'd just heard. Big Hair was Will Faraday's mother, Sissy Rae's grandmother. And Will was Sissy Rae's father, not to mention Violet Comstock's ex-husband. Which meant the story Violet had told Consuela about Sissy Rae's father being found dead in a Chicago homeless shelter was total bull.

I blinked, trying to picture easygoing, down-to-earth Will married to bossy, self-impressed Violet. It wasn't easy. As if reading my mind, Will hung his head and said, "I guess I was blinded by her beauty. Love can really mess with your mind."

Captain Nishio frowned. "If you're telling the truth, we can't return Sissy Rae to her mother. Unfortunately, I can't give her to you either. No matter how noble your intentions, Mr. Faraday, you have broken the law and must be taken to jail. Sissy Rae will be put in foster care until the courts decide where she belongs."

"But can't Will hold Sissy Rae, at least until we get to the police station?" I asked. "I mean, look at her. She's miserable."

We all turned to Sissy Rae, who was blubbering and reaching out her arms to Will. "Daddy!" she wailed, struggling to escape from the female police officer who was holding her. "I want my daddy!"

Nishio thought it over. "All right. You can hold her while we drive to the station." He called to the officer, who brought Sissy Rae over. Nishio used the handcuffs to lock Will's right hand to the door handle. His other hand was left free to hold Sissy Rae in his lap. The little girl snuggled against his chest and instantly stopped crying.

Nishio started the police car. As we drove away, I turned to look out the rear window. A crowd had gathered to see what was going on. Some city workers were turning off the water, and a tow truck had arrived to take Will's pickup away. As I watched, the driver retrieved Jackson's bike and heaved it into the front seat of his truck.

I sighed, wondering what had become of my bike. It had probably been run over by a car after I ditched it in the middle of Hill Street. Oddly enough, the thought made me sad. I'd been dying to buy a new, ultra-hot mountain bike for months, but now—well, I guess I hadn't realized until just that minute how attached I was to my old cruiser.

Will's voice brought me back to the present. "I had no idea where Violet had taken Sissy Rae, not a clue where to look. I just couldn't believe she'd pick up and move out here. She didn't know a soul in Hollywood, and she didn't have two nickels to rub together."

"How did you find out she was here?" Nishio asked.

"It was me who seen her," Sissy Rae's grandmother said, pushing her limp hair out of her eyes. "I turned on the TV back at my house in Arkansas, and there was my granddaughter hawking toilet paper. I was so startled I almost fell off my Barcalounger! Soon as the commercial ended, I ran to the phone and called Sonny in Iowa. The next day we were on our way out here."

"When we got here, I began askin' around about Violet," Will explained. "I found out where she lived and started followin' her and Sissy Rae." He hugged his daughter, who was dozing in his lap, a look of contentment on her freckled face. "It didn't take me long to figure out that my little girl was unhappy. She didn't have any playmates, not even any time to play. Violet had her taking lessons and going to auditions all day long."

"I knew that hussy wasn't going to let us take Sissy Rae back home," Grandma broke in. "And we couldn't afford a lawyer to take her to court."

"Besides, legal battles like that can drag on for years," Will said. "I wanted my baby back right away, before Hollywood corrupted her. So I decided to kidnap her. I know it was wrong, but I was a desperate man."

"Only we couldn't get near her," Grandma went on. "Violet made sure Sissy Rae was never out of her sight. Then one day I was watchin' that TV show *L.A. Your Way,* and I seen that Sissy Rae had eaten at Baby Bistro—with Violet in the other room."

Will turned to me. "So I went to your parents' restaurant, hopin' to land a job there so I could get close to Sissy Rae. It was just dumb luck that Jean-Michel had quit the night before and your mama was looking for a new assistant chef."

130

"But how did you know when Sissy Rae would come back to Baby Bistro?" Jackson asked.

"I didn't," Will answered. "I just watched and waited. And prayed."

"I kept the pickup truck parked at the end of the alley every night, just in case Violet and Sissy Rae returned," Grandma said. "The night Violet finally showed up again, Will ran outside and told me. I poked my head in the baby room five or six times, waitin' for a chance to whisk her out of there."

I thought back to the night of the kidnapping, trying to remember if I'd seen Sissy Rae's grandmother in the restaurant. Suddenly it all came back to me. I'd seen a woman with a huge bouffant hairdo walk into the baby room just a few minutes before I took Sissy Rae to the bathroom. Little had I known that it was Sissy Rae's grandmother come to kidnap her granddaughter!

"Finally, I saw my chance," she said, pointing at me. "I saw this boy here take Sissy Rae to the bathroom, and then I saw him leave her there and go into the other bathroom. I ran out to the pickup truck and drove it into the alley. Then I climbed up on the hood and opened the bathroom window. When Sissy Rae saw me, she untied her sash and scrambled right up on the back of the toilet, and I pulled her outside."

"And you started that kitchen fire to distract everyone's attention," Captain Nishio said, looking at Will in the rearview mirror. "Am I correct, Mr. Faraday?"

"Not quite," he replied. "The soufflé fire was a bonafide accident. But I faked the cough so Puck's mama would let me leave early. Then I snuck around to the front of the restaurant, went inside, and locked the bathroom window. I left the note, too. I'd pasted it together days before, using a letter from Pearl Pendergast that I snitched from Violet's car."

Everything was falling into place. "Then you sneaked into Pearl Pendergast's office and left Sissy Rae's diaper bag behind her desk in order to make the cops suspicious," I said. "Right?"

Will nodded. "I'd just dropped it off when you ran into me in the lobby of Pearl's office building. My mama was the one who tipped off the police." He turned to me, his basset-hound face looking even more haggard than usual. "I never wanted to get your family in trouble, Puck. You're good people. That's why I tried to make it look like Pearl had kidnapped Sissy Rae."

"Then why did you deliver a second note to Violet using scraps of paper with Mr. Rosen's handwriting on them?" Jackson asked accusingly.

Will's face fell. "No one seemed to suspect Pearl, despite all my hard work. The papers never wrote anything about her. All they seemed to care about was Puck and his family."

"That's because Pearl Pendergast has been a top Hollywood agent since the early days of television," Captain Nishio explained. "She's got this town in her back pocket, the media included. So the tabloids went after the Rosens instead."

"I was frightened," Will went on. "Captain Nishio was coming around my apartment, asking tough questions. Plus, you boys were snooping around, looking for evidence."

"So one day I chased you in my truck," Sissy Rae's grandmother said. "I just wanted to give you a little scare."

"That wasn't my idea," Will said. "You've got to forgive my mama. She gets a little carried away sometimes."

"What's the big deal?" Grandma asked. "I didn't hurt them, did I?"

Will didn't answer. "I knew I had to get out of town, and fast," he said. "So I stole a handwritten letter from Mr.

Rosen's office and pasted the letters onto the kidnapping note. I figured the cops wouldn't really be able to pin anything on him, but it would buy me some time while I packed up the truck and took off."

"But why did you bother to come to work today?" I asked. "Why didn't you just take Sissy Rae and disappear?"

"That's what *I* asked him," Grandma said irritably. "Why take chances? Get while the gettin's good, that's my motto."

"I couldn't leave without saying good-bye," Will insisted. "Puck's mama took a chance on me, givin' me a job I really wasn't qualified for. I wanted us to part company on good terms."

I looked at Will, sitting there with his arm wrapped protectively around Sissy Rae. I couldn't really be mad at him. Sure, he'd broken the law, and he'd caused a lot of trouble for my family. Still, everything he'd done had been to help his daughter. How could I fault him for that?

The police station was up ahead. Apparently the news of Will's arrest had traveled fast, because the parking lot was filled with reporters, photographers, TV cameramen, and dozens upon dozens of curiosity seekers. As Captain Nishio pulled into the driveway, they surrounded us, snapping photos and shouting questions.

"How does it feel to be heroes, boys?" a reporter called through the window.

I looked at Jackson. Heroes? Is that what we were? It didn't feel that way, not since we'd heard Will's story. Now it seemed that Will was the hero, and we were the bad guys. Thanks to us, Sissy Rae and her father were about to be separated once again. Thanks to us, Will Faraday and his mother were about to go to jail.

I wondered if Jackson felt the same way I did, but before

133

I could ask him, four police officers hurried out of the station to escort us inside. As they opened the car doors, I stepped out and turned to the crowd of reporters. "Will Faraday isn't a kidnapper," I announced. "He's Sissy Rae's father, and he was trying to take her back to Iowa so she could have a normal life."

"What about the kid's mother?" a reporter called. "Doesn't she have custody of Sissy Rae?"

"Not anymore," Jackson answered. "Anyway, if you ask me, Sissy Rae belongs with her father. He's the one who really loves her."

So Jackson *did* feel the same as me. I grinned and slapped him a high five. Then the officers took our arms and bustled us through the crowd. I was heading up the steps to the station when I heard a familiar voice. "Uck coming! Hi, Uck! Hi!"

I looked up to see my little sister standing in the doorway. Behind her stood my mother and father, and next to them were Jackson's parents. Before I could take another step, Mom ran forward and grabbed me in a suffocating bear hug. "Oh, Puck," she cried, "thank goodness you're all right!"

"I'm fine," I said, struggling to breathe. "Come on, Mom, knock it off. People are taking our picture."

I twisted out of her arms and saw that Jackson was having the same problem with his mother. "Relax, Mom, I'm okay," he said. "Puck's the one who got cut up."

"Cut up!" my mother shrieked, noticing my knees for the first time. "Oh, my poor baby!"

Before I could reply, Will came up the stairs. One of his hands was handcuffed to Captain Nishio, and the other still held Sissy Rae against his chest. Behind him came Sissy Rae's grandmother with two police officers gripping her arms. We all stepped inside the station. Then Captain Nishio turned to Will.

"Time to hand her over," he said.

Will looked like he was about to cry. Nishio reached out for Sissy Rae, but she threw her arms around her father's neck and held on for dear life. "Come on, Sissy Rae, it's okay," Will said, trying to sound cheerful. "Go to the nice man."

"Want Daddy!" she sobbed, holding him tighter. "Want Daddy!"

Poor Sissy Rae, I thought. And then I had an idea. "Why does Sissy Rae have to go into foster care?" I asked. "Why can't she stay with my family?"

"You want to take Sissy Rae?" Jackson asked with disbelief. "I thought you couldn't stand toddlers."

"Babies are pretty cool," I said with a shrug, and I meant it. Thanks to my job at Baby Bistro and my friendship with Will, I'd learned to understand little kids, and even— wonder of wonders—to sort of like them.

Besides, Sissy Rae's tear-stained face made me think of Julia. "I wouldn't want *my* baby sister to go through what Sissy Rae's been through," I said. I turned to my parents. "Can we take care of her? Please?"

Mom and Dad looked at each other. "It's all right with us," Dad said, "but what does the law say?" He turned to Captain Nishio. "Can we be Sissy Rae's legal guardians until the court decides what's best for her?"

A small smile spread across the detective's stonelike face. "Call me tomorrow," he said.

Chapter
15

"Ladies and gentlemen, boys and girls," Dad announced, cutting the red ribbon that was tied across the front door of the restaurant, "Baby Bistro is now officially reopened!"

Cameras clicked and reporters scribbled notes as the first customers streamed into the restaurant. Dad was beaming as he opened his reservation book, and Mom's eyes glowed brightly. She gave Dad a kiss on the cheek, then hurried off to the kitchen.

Jackson and I slapped each other a proud high five. After all, we'd had a hand in the reopening of Baby Bistro. Ever since we found Sissy Rae, the public had viewed us as heroes. We'd been interviewed on TV, written up in the newspapers, even mentioned in a couple of national magazines.

Thanks to all the publicity, the bank had loaned my parents enough money to reopen the restaurant. The phone had been ringing off the hook ever since with people wanting reservations. Baby Bistro was hot again.

Jackson and I took our places in the baby room. Julia and Sissy Rae were already there, playing at the toy box with Julia's baby doll, Loola. It was hard to believe, but almost an entire month had passed since Sissy Rae had come to stay with us. It had taken a lot of phone calls and paperwork to make it happen, but it had definitely been worth it.

I watched as Sissy Rae happily ran a comb through Loola's tangled hair. Gone was the whiny little girl with the perfectly combed hair and spotless dresses. In her place was the new Sissy Rae—messy hair, untied shoelaces, and a big grin on her dirty face.

I slipped into my apron as the first baby diners toddled through the door. It didn't take long for things to return to normal. Kids were crying and smearing food in their hair, rich and famous parents were demanding special treatment, and Jackson and I were making total fools of ourselves trying to keep the grown-ups and their little darlings happy.

"How about a chorus of 'Greasy, Grimy Gopher Guts'?" Jackson suggested as he pulled a celery stick out of a toddler's nose.

I let out a groan. "I was hoping I'd never have to hear that song again."

"Hey, what happened to the new Puck Rosen?" he asked. "The one who adores babies?"

"Don't misquote me," I said. "I hardly ever want to put Julia in the trash compactor these days, but that doesn't mean I'm baby-crazy. Any way you slice it, a roomful of hungry toddlers is no picnic."

As if to prove my point, a grumpy-looking one-year-old puked strained sweet potatoes all over my shoes. I did a slow burn and Jackson cracked up. "Don't let it get to you," he said, handing me a wet wipe from his apron pocket. "Remember, there's more to life than Baby Bistro. Think mountain biking!"

I grinned. We had spent the last few weeks working on

our ultimate mountain biking course. All we needed were a couple more moguls and we'd be ready to rip. But that wasn't the only reason to be happy.

Will Faraday's case had gone to court the week before, and Mom and Dad had testified on his behalf. It had taken only a few more witnesses—Consuela, Sissy Rae's dance instructor, the director of the Puff 'N' Soft Toilet Tissue commercial—to convince the judge that Violet had pushed Sissy Rae into show business against her father's wishes and that being forced to perform was against her best interests.

After all the evidence was in, the judge gave Will and his mother suspended sentences and ordered them to get six months of counseling and do two hundred hours of community service. During their probation they'd be allowed to spend three hours a day with Sissy Rae. When it ended, they could have her back for good.

Violet Comstock wasn't so lucky. She had been convicted of kidnapping and given a one-year sentence. When she was released from jail, she was supposed to attend counseling sessions. If and when she was judged capable of being a fit mother to Sissy Rae, she was to be given limited visiting privileges.

"Good news, guys," Dad announced, strolling into the baby room. "Will just called to congratulate us on the reopening of the restaurant. He and his mother are being released from jail next week. I offered him his old job back, and he accepted." He smiled with satisfaction. "Pretty soon everything will be back to normal around here."

"Not quite," I pointed out. "School starts in two weeks, and, well, Jackson and I are going to be kind of busy, Dad."

"I already thought of that," he replied. "I hired two out-of-work comedians to take over your jobs during the week.

But I'd still like you to work on weekends. After all, you're a big part of why Baby Bistro is so successful."

With two toddlers at home to deal with, I wasn't so sure I wanted to keep working at the restaurant, even if it was only part-time. But Jackson didn't wait to hear my opinion. "We'll do it," he said. "*If* we get a raise, that is. Plus, two twenty-minute breaks every evening, and all the Triple-Mondo-Mega Cheeseburgers we can eat."

Dad laughed and shook his head. "You drive a hard bargain, but . . . well, okay. You got it."

All the Triple-Mondo-Mega Cheeseburgers I could eat? How could I say no to that? Anyway, I was starting to enjoy the concept of making money. Over the summer I'd saved almost six hundred dollars. That was practically enough to buy a Cheetah 2000.

Dad left, and Jackson and I turned back to the babies. Now Sissy Rae got into the act, demanding a dish of spinach with chocolate sauce.

"And a spicy cheesewich!" Julia cried.

I groaned. Ever since Sissy Rae had come to live with us, Julia had decided that she liked weird food combinations, too. Spicy-cheese ice cream sandwiches were her latest.

"All right," I said, making a face. I turned to find a busboy and instead found Pearl Pendergast striding toward me with a tall, silver-haired man at her side. It took me a second to realize that I knew him. He was Mr. Calhoun, the owner of Calhoun's Kooky Cookies.

"At last I've found you!" he cried, grabbing my hand and pumping it up and down. "And you!" he added, motioning to Jackson, who was across the room wiping tomato soup off a sticky toddler. "Come over here, young man!"

Jackson walked up, and Mr. Calhoun threw his arms around our shoulders. "Ever since that day I saw you in

Pearl's office, I knew you were the perfect boys for my new Kooky Cookies commercial. You've got personality, sincerity, charm . . ."

"They're real All-American boys," Pearl cooed in her gravelly voice. She grabbed our cheeks and pinched them hard.

I stared at her. Last time we'd seen her, she'd threatened us with her Dragon Lady claws. But now that there was money to be made, she was acting like our biggest fan.

I guess Pearl knew what I was thinking because she lit a cigarette and said, "I should be mad at you for reuniting my biggest client with her show biz–hating father, but what the heck? I've got a forgiving nature." She spotted Sissy Rae across the room and waved broadly. "Hi, sweetie! Remember Auntie Pearl?"

Sissy Rae responded by bursting into tears. Mr. Calhoun didn't seem to notice. "Of course, I told myself to forget about you boys," he continued. "You were juvenile delinquents. Troublemakers. Not the kind of kids I wanted representing my Kooky Cookies."

"But then one day Mr. Calhoun turned on the TV, and there you were on the news," Pearl continued. "You had risked your lives to find Sissy Rae, the announcer said. You were heroes!"

I shrugged. "We were just trying to help," I said.

"Hear that, Pearl? They're modest, too!" Mr. Calhoun exclaimed. He turned back to us. "So I went to Pearl and demanded to know your names. That's when she told me you weren't juvenile delinquents after all. You're normal, well-adjusted boys, just like I thought in the first place."

"Handsome, too," Pearl said, grabbing my chin and twisting my head. "Just look at that profile."

"So whaddaya say, boys?" Mr. Calhoun asked. "Will you

star in my new commercial? I'll pay you ten thousand bucks each, plus residuals."

"Ten thousand bucks!" Jackson gasped. "What do we have to do?"

"Just be yourselves. And, of course, let us film you eating and enjoying Calhoun's Kooky Cookies."

Jackson grinned. "We could do that in our sleep. Right, Puck?"

I didn't answer right away. I'd never had the slightest desire to be in a TV commercial. But then no one had ever offered me ten thousand dollars before. I pictured all the things I could buy with that kind of money. "Well, sure," I began. "I mean—"

"Absolutely not," Pearl broke in, facing off with Mr. Calhoun. "Who do you think you're dealing with? Nobodies? My clients are heroes. They wouldn't even consider doing your commercial for less than twenty thousand."

If Mr. Calhoun was bothered by Pearl's change of attitude, he didn't show it. I guess he was used to dealing with Hollywood agents. "It's a deal!" he crowed, slapping our backs. "I'll call your parents in the morning and give them all the details. We can meet in Pearl's office tomorrow afternoon to sign the contracts." We all shook hands, and Pearl and Mr. Calhoun walked out of the baby room arm in arm.

After that, the evening seemed to fly by. I kept thinking about the twenty thousand dollars Mr. Calhoun was going to pay me and planning what I was going to buy with it. By the time Dad escorted the last customers out the front door, I had it all figured out.

"What a night!" Dad said, as we trooped into Baby Bistro's kitchen. Mom was waiting with slices of chocolate mousse cake for Dad, Jackson, and me, and homemade lollipops for Julia and Sissy Rae.

"You don't know the half of it," I said. Quickly, Jackson and I explained about the Kooky Cookie commercial.

"Well, what do you think, Puck?" Mom asked when we were finished talking. "You've seen the dark side of child stardom this summer. Are you sure you're ready to become an actor?"

I shrugged. "I'm not looking for a career," I said, "but one commercial might be kind of fun."

"It won't really be acting anyway," Jackson pointed out. "We really *do* like Calhoun's Kooky Cookies."

Dad smiled. "If you want to do it, I say go for it. But don't think you're going to get star treatment at home. No matter how famous you become, you'll still have to take out the trash and make your bed."

"I promise," I answered.

I looked down at Sissy Rae, contentedly licking her lollipop. Like Mom said, I'd seen what the pressures of show business could do to a kid, and believe me, I had no desire to live that kind of life. Just dealing with all the media attention I'd received over the summer had been hard enough. I mean, being a celebrity *was* exciting. But the truth is, I was happy just being plain old Puck Rosen—mountain biker, big brother, and regular kid.

"Just think, boys," Dad remarked, pouring himself a cup of coffee, "after you do this commercial you'll have enough money to buy new mountain bikes and still put something away toward your college education."

I pictured my old cruiser. Turns out the police had found it in the gutter on Hill Street. After Jackson had escaped from the motorcycle cops (by faking an asthma attack and then kicking one of them in the knee), he had managed to rescue my bike from the heavy traffic before hopping on his own and coming to *my* rescue.

"You know, I'm not so sure I need a new bike," I said.

"But I thought you were dying for a Cougar 200!" Mom exclaimed.

"A Cheetah 2000," I corrected her. "And yes, I was. But now I'm wondering, what's the point? I mean, my old bike performed great when we were chasing Will—except on that tight cutback, of course. But a new Blastmaster Brand suspension fork would take care of that."

"I know what you mean," Jackson said. "If our bikes can handle rush-hour traffic in downtown L.A., I figure they can handle pretty much anything."

I nodded. "Besides, ever since the newspapers printed all those photos of Captain Nishio returning our mountain bikes to us, the bikes are practically as famous as we are. It would seem kind of disloyal to get rid of them."

"Wonderful," Dad said. "That means you can put all the money from the Kooky Cookie commercial into your college fund."

"Hang on," I said. "I think I deserve to spend part of the money any way I choose."

"What did you have in mind?" Mom asked.

"I thought I'd get one of those baby bike seats, the kind you bolt on behind the seat of an adult bicycle. And a baby bike helmet, too." Mom and Dad looked stunned—and Jackson looked pretty startled, too—but I just grinned. "Hey, why not? I figure it's about time I introduced my little sister to the joys of biking."

"Me, too!" Sissy Rae pleaded. "Me, too!"

I looked at Jackson. "How about it? You could put a baby seat on your bike and bring Sissy Rae along, too."

He thought it over. "Can we take them off-road?"

"If you're very careful," Dad said. "But no wild maneuvers. Remember, these are toddlers we're talking about."

Julia jumped to her feet and hugged me around the legs, plastering her half-eaten lollipop against my jeans. "Bike, Uck!" she squealed. "Zoom! Zoom!"

I laughed and lifted her into my arms. "That's right," I said, smiling into her sticky face. "Uck and Julia are going to go zoom—together!"